Flying Through Music

Flying Through Music

Susan Zeidler

Wasteland Press
Shelbyville, KY USA
www.wastelandpress.net

Flying Through Music
by Susan Zeidler

First Printing – June 2012
ISBN: 978-1-60047-732-4

Flying Through Music is a work of fiction, and the names and characters are the product of the author's imagination. If any of those names resemble real people, their creation is coincidental and unintentional. Although some real historical events, institutions and famous individuals are mentioned, all are used fictitiously.

Printed in the U.S.A.

0   1   2   3   4   5   6   7   8   9   10   11   12   13

*For my father David Zeidler,
a pilot and the inspiration for this book.*

ACKNOWLEDGEMENTS

To David Evans, my husband and navigator. To Betty Zeidler, my amazing mom. To Rachel Evans, my incredible daughter. To Steven, Larry, Denise, Serena, Sari, Melissa, Danny, Richard, my fabulous fam. To my beautiful Baldwin buddies Mindy Ellenberg Slater, who always makes me laugh and inspires me with her strength, Michele Kraushaar and Debbie Lichliter, for showing up when I needed them. To Renee Greenberg for her chicken soup. To Barry Rosenbloom and all the wonderful people at Tower. To Jo Furman, my gentle rock of Gibraltar. To Independent Writers of Southern California (IWOSC) and the Society of Children's Book Writers and Illustrators (SCBWI), great writer groups. To Reuters News and the talented Los Angeles bureau. To editors Kelly Luce and Chris Eboch. To Timothy Renfrow at Wasteland Press, a wonderful advocate. To all my phenomenal relatives and friends for making every day a gift. To passionate musicians and pilots who love what they do.

CHAPTER ONE

Hole in the Sky

The C note started pounding so loudly in my ear that it drowned out everything. The cheering fans, the roar of the engines, the air show announcer.

"Nathan's coming soon," said my best friend Tammy, but the rest of her sentence was muted by the D chord that was now going off in my head.

It was a hot August day, and we were in Oshkosh, Wisconsin, at one of the biggest air shows in the world. We were in the bleachers near a runway to see our friend Nathan perform in an air demonstration. He'd be flying a brand new plane called a Silo. Nathan's girlfriend, Ruby, sat between us.

Tammy had met Nathan and Ruby the previous summer. I had just met them in the last few hours. It was my first time at the air show. Tammy had been going to Oshkosh since she was a little kid. Her dad was a pilot.

"What time is….," said Ruby. But I couldn't hear anything she was saying. All I could do was read her lips. An F major chord rang through my brain. This was getting old. I should've seen it coming. Why hadn't I recognized the signs as soon as I heard the first note? I must've been in denial.

I had just assumed the sounds had something to do with the Midwest, or being surrounded by all these airplanes, or some mechanism in the air traffic control system. After all, I'd never been to an air show before.

I used to think of kids' overalls or cheese when I'd hear someone say Oshkosh. But each summer, about a million people visit Oshkosh and the fields around Wittman Regional Airport were transformed into a giant campground. People pitched tents right under their planes and settled in. It was a flier's paradise.

The sky was ablaze with an airborne carnival of colorful airplanes and skydivers. Planes flew in formation. Pilots walked on wings and old-fashioned biplanes did aerobatics.

And there was a great "Fly Market" on the grounds with all sorts of aviation-themed things. Tammy bought me a really cute set of pajamas made from a parachute! How cool is that? And there were concerts and parties.

"What time is….," said Tammy, but her words just faded into the F chord ringing through my brain. A long-forgotten sensation began to stir inside of me, but I shrugged it off. It couldn't be. Not again.

"Ladies and gentlemen," the announcer said. His booming voice was loud and clear to the crowd but to me it was muffled. It sounded like he was talking through one of those tin can telephones you make with a string when you learn about sound vibrations.

"We have a great show today!" he bellowed.

Ruby gripped my hand, which caught me by surprise. I barely knew her. She looked really nervous. Why? Didn't Nathan do this all the time?

"Are you okay?" I asked not able to hear my own words. Ruby didn't seem to either, but I doubted it was because a D chord was blasting through her brain.

Her mind was somewhere else as she gazed down the runway to where Nathan's plane stood waiting to taxi.

Nathan wore many hats but they all involved flying. He was a flight instructor, a charter pilot and a crop duster. He said he'd done demos like this before, but was super excited that Cougar Aviation had asked him to demonstrate the Silo.

The money was nice too. They were paying him five thousand dollars. "I'm taking all you gals out for a fine dinner," he had promised earlier that day.

The faint sounds of military music brought me back to the present. Nathan began taxiing the plane.

"Here it is!" cried the announcer. I glanced over at Ruby. She looked freaked. Maybe she always got like this when Nathan was performing. I wanted to ease her mind somehow, but my own brain felt like an acoustical chamber filled with chord tones.

A B minor 7th chord echoed like a giant church organ. It grew louder with each second, drumming out everything else. Neither the loudspeaker, the thousands of excited people nor the roar of the engine were competition for that chord in my brain.

The chords were beginning to freak me out, especially the creepy-sounding minor ones that reminded me of a horror movie soundtrack. And all of a sudden, I had a nagging feeling that something terrible was about to happen.

When I look back at that air show, I think of it in slow motion.

I see it frame by frame, with new details emerging clearer each time. It hurts me to think of it. I wish I could forget it. But I can't and never will.

The worst part about it was the helplessness. I felt completely and utterly helpless. I was unable to stop the music from running through my head at that most maddening moment as a horrible sight unfolded before my eyes.

Nobody but Ruby and I thought anything was wrong. I looked around the crowd and saw eager excitement on people's faces. Maybe Ruby and I were being ridiculous, I thought, as Nathan's plane taxied down the runway.

Moments later, he accelerated, lifted the nose and climbed upwards in a perfectly normal take-off.

Ruby still held my hand but her grip relaxed as Nathan's path of flight appeared normal. She watched the Silo as it looped gracefully in the sky. Jazzy music offered a nice soundtrack to the plane stunts and the chords in my head finally started to feel like they were in sync with the rest of the world, like a tight rhythm section.

The crowd applauded. Ruby let go of my hand to clap too. She smiled, looking relieved.

But sadly, this relief was premature. It was right at that point when the trouble began. And all it took was two minutes.

In two minutes, a thousand or so people's lives were changed. Up in the sky Nathan's plane began to hiccup. At first, the crowd thought it was another stunt and they cheered. But Ruby sat very still. In my brain, an E chord started chirping in staccato fashion, giving me a headache just as I saw that something was very, very wrong.

The plane sputtered some more.

Then the crowd grew quiet. People squinted upward curiously. Some began to murmur. Everyone was realizing that something was not right. And then, something so bizarre happened that it would forever confound any scholar in the subject of aviation.

The heavens would betray Nathan like others before him who had lost their lives in pursuit of the dream of flight. But no pilot had ever perished in quite the same way.

People who saw what happened next would never forget it. Radio talk shows would devote hours to it. College courses would be built around it.

That's because there's never been an official explanation. All people know is that Nathan's plane began to shake and shake. It trembled so violently that after half a minute, it grew blurry and then blurrier. And then something unfathomable happened.

In that one horrible moment, Nathan became a statistic and an enigma. Nathan didn't crash into a mountain, the ground or even a body of water. His plane didn't explode into smithereens after ramming into a foreign object, nor was it struck by lightning or a piece of ammunition.

Nathan's plane just simply disappeared. It was gone, just like that. In the blink of an eye, the crowd heard a little sizzle resembling the sound of an electric bug zapper and then it saw the plane disintegrate into a purple puff of smoke.

No one said anything. It was so quiet you could hear a pin drop. Even the chords in my brain had finally stopped.

And then, Ruby shrieked.

CHAPTER TWO

Flight and Music

My name is Zoey Browne and three years ago, my life was normal. Well, normal for someone who was the daughter of a workaholic single mother and a guy who disappeared before I was born.

But that all changed when I was 12 and discovered I was a musiator. What's a musiator? It's a kind of hybrid musical aviator. This is a story about flight and music. I've discovered that pilots and musicians actually have a lot in common. Both are born with a talent that flows through their veins. The urge to fly or make music is so powerful, it's as if it's embedded in one's DNA

Sadly, sometimes the two worlds collide in tragedy. Some of the greatest musicians who lived have died in flight. But their sound remains for generations to enjoy. I found this out in sometimes painful ways during that summer of Nathan's disappearance.

I fly too, but not like other pilots. I am a musiator and I musi-morph. I travel through time when I study music. Instead of practicing rhythm, harmony and melody with a book or a teacher and then applying those skills to an instrument, I actually BECOME the musical trait.

Once, when I was studying rhythm, for instance, my whole body pulsated like a giant metronome for days. But it's even crazier than that because when this happens, I also travel to another world. It's like time travelling and metamorphosis all rolled into one.

The place I go to is called Musicland. It's a magical, otherworldly place. And it's never the same. Every time I go there, Musicland transforms itself into different locales and times in history that relate to the musical element I'm studying.

I have musi-morphed to Harlem, New York in the 1930s, the Titanic in 1912, Woodstock in 1969 and the fall of the Berlin Wall in 1989.

There are others like me. I can sometimes sense when someone is a musiator, but we're not supposed to talk about it. If you break this rule, you may never go to this magical musical universe again.

When Nathan's plane went down, I hadn't musi-morphed in three years. I almost wondered if I had violated the rule of silence, not that I remembered doing so. I wasn't worried, though, because so much else had happened that I barely missed it. And maybe I just didn't need to time travel anymore.

People who musi-morph are highly musical and are usually seeking answers about their past. But when I musi-morphed three years ago, I solved the big mystery in my life. I found my dad.

Mom had thought Dad was dead, but I never did. And when I musi-morphed, I discovered he was very much alive. It's complicated. But basically, he had gotten sick and suffered amnesia. Dad had wandered around the country with a different identity and that's why we didn't know he was alive.

Now my life's totally different. Well, for one, I'm the daughter of a famous rock star. My dad is the legendary David Peer. And he's a really cool guy too. I still live with Mom in Los Angeles but he visits us all the time between his shows and recording sessions. And for the past three summers, I've gone on tour with him and his band.

The other big change has to do with me. Before all this happened, I was sort of a beige kid. I was blocked, never felt good at anything. But through musi-morphing, I found my music.

I'm still the same old Zoey. I'll never be the most popular or funniest kid in school, but I don't care. Up until this summer, I'd never even had a boyfriend, which is so lame. But I'm a mean keyboard player and that's what counts. I'm getting better on the piano all the time.

I'm in a jazz workshop at school and it's a blast. There's so much music in me that's just dying to get out, I can't wait every day for the moment that I'm sitting in front of a piano and playing. I can honestly say it's truly great when you find something you love to do.

So I didn't think I needed to musi-morph to find answers. I knew where I had to go and it was to the white and black keys right at my fingertips. I had a lifetime of musical journeying ahead to keep me busy.

Or so I thought until that summer and the air show. In Oshkosh, musi-morphing came back into my life. This time, it wasn't pulling me to that alternative universe to find my own answers. I would soon realize that I was destined to use these strange and wonderful powers to help others find their answers, sometimes going to dark, sad places in search of difficult truths.

I guess you could say I'd become a sort of musical sleuth.

I hadn't even planned to go to Oshkosh that summer. When my life zigzagged musically once again, I was with my dad in Chicago on a fifteen-city tour. We'd already been to Miami, Atlanta and New York. Some other Midwestern cities were up next before we returned to California in the fall.

I was backstage at the Wrigley Theatre in Chicago, listening to Dad sing his hit song "Rodney." I watched the crew waiting in the wings for Dad to finish so they could tear down the set. After his encores, Dad came backstage to find me.

"You ready to get something to eat?" he asked. He's one of the nicest guys I know on top of being really famous.

The only problem is that EVERYBODY loves my dad and it's beginning to get old. I'm just getting to know him myself and I'm already seeing the downside to having a rock dad. You can never have him all to yourself.

It's not his fault really, I thought, staring at him. Women especially fell for his dark hair and bright blue eyes.

People say I resemble him. Our faces are the same shape now that I've shed some baby fat. But I don't think I'm half as attractive as he is handsome. It's amazing how all the catty girls who used to taunt me for being chubby started kissing up to me after they found out David Peer was my dad!

I would say that music's the only thing that's ever been consistent in Dad's life -- until now. Rock and roll kept him going all these years. He hardly notices the commotion in the world around him because there's a constant soundtrack always running through his head. I guess I've inherited his musical genes.

Dad was always a lone wolf. But now things were different with mom and me in his life. And so he thought going on tour together would be a way of getting closer. I didn't want to burst Dad's bubble, but being on the road with a rock band doesn't quite cut it as traditional father-daughter time. But that's okay. I've never had it too normal anyway, so this felt right to me. Or did it?

"I'm starving," I said, smiling back at him.

We started walking back towards his dressing room. "Great show!" said Dad's bass player Derek as he passed us, grabbing Dad in a bear hug.

"See you at the airport tomorrow morning dude," said my father as he pulled away. Ouch. We had a 9 am flight to Pittsburgh. It just wasn't doing it for me. I didn't mean to complain. Staying in all these nice hotels and being backstage for these shows was great, but I was beginning to see the problems that came with stardom. Having people in my face all the time was getting old. Sometimes it felt like I was spending more time backstage with the crew and the handlers than with my own father. Could I be growing jaded so fast? Or was I just getting lonely being the only kid on the tour?

I pushed aside these feelings as we arrived at Dad's dressing room and he put his arm around me. He looked so happy. "I'll take a quick shower. Then let's go out to eat. I know a great ribs place!"

As I waited I felt my cell phone vibrate, signalling a text message. I pulled it out of my pocket and saw that Tammy had been trying to call me during the concert.

"In Oshkosh! Really close to Chicago. Come to air show 4 a few days? We have room in the tent."

I pictured Tammy at the air show. It would be so much fun to see her. I missed her. We never got to hang out now that we were in different high schools. And she'd been talking about the Oshkosh Fly-in for years. It would be nice to get away from the chaos of the tour for a few days.

But these images faded as my phone started to ring.

It was Mom. "Hi Zoey. How was the show?"

"Great! They did a killer version of 'Landscaper.' Everyone was standing for the entire show," I replied.

"I wish I could be there," she said with longing in her voice, sounding more like a star-struck girl than a history professor. Who was this person, I wondered? I'd never seen her in love. It had always been just me and her.

I'd had a great childhood. Mom had done everything for me single-handedly. She never showed an interest in dating anyone. I guess she never stopped loving my dad even if she did think he was dead.

And now that we had found him, she'd fallen in love with my father all over again. And he had fallen in love with her. Sometimes I thought they were trying too hard to make up for lost time, though.

Mom came along with us for part of the tour before she had to head back for the summer session. And Dad was planning on living with us in the fall. Poor guy, he'd never had a home. He'd been on the road all of his life, like a gypsy. He was really looking forward to settling in with us. It was going to be interesting.

"I wish you were here too, Mom," I said, surprised by my words. Was I really missing her? I mean, who wouldn't want to trade places with me in an instant and tour with a rock band?

As I hung up, Dad came out with wet hair, a fresh shirt and jeans on.

"Ready to eat?" he asked.

"Sure," I said.

We ate tons of barbecue in a downtown blues bar. It was so dark that we figured nobody would recognize Dad. But as usual, that was not the case.

As I was digging into my fourth baby back, a forty-something with helmet hair and a tight skirt came sauntering over to our table.

"David, dear!" she said slipping my dad a business card. "My name's Daisy and I'm a singer. I can't believe you're here at TJs! I was just at your show!" she said bending over and wagging her gigantic breasts right in Dad's face.

I nearly gagged on my rib. Most fans were really nice, but once in a while, an oddball came along and it really creeped me out. No fun. It just made me want to stay home. This kind of thing had happened before and was beginning to get on my nerves.

Dad didn't seem to mind Daisy too much. He had more patience with big-boobed boobs than I did.

"Can I sit with you two for a while?" she asked. I shot my dad a look that said I'd kill if he said yes, but before he could even answer her, Daisy had sat down.

Luckily for me, my cell phone began to vibrate again, which gave me an excuse to leave the table.

"Ummm. I'll be right back Dad. I have to see who this is," I said waving the phone in front of Daisy's face. "Nice meeting you Daisy." I walked outside the restaurant into the warm Chicago night air.

Tammy was texting me again. I had forgotten all about her earlier message.

"Why haven't you answered? Can you come to the air show?"

I texted her back**: "Would love to. I'll ask dad."**

I walked back into the restaurant feeling excited but my enthusiasm waned when I saw that Daisy was still at the table. She was probably the most annoying person I'd ever met. I sat there and sulked while she and Dad gabbed over the music. Finally, after another set, we paid the bill and started to leave.

"Please call me any time you're in the Windy City!" said Daisy, shoving her chest in my father's face again. I wanted to throw up.

"Thanks Daisy! I'll be recording a new album in Los Angeles after this tour, but you never know when I'll wind up back in Chicago."

He really didn't get it. He was so clueless about fathering that he didn't realize he shouldn't be flirting with groupies in front of his daughter. I was getting angrier and angrier. Heck, he shouldn't flirt with groupies period if he was really serious about my mother.

He finally noticed my foul mood. "Sorry about that," he said.

"What are you sorry about?"

"I guess I shouldn't have let her sit at our table."

I checked out his face to see if he was for real. He seemed to mean it, but this was not the first time it had happened so I didn't really believe it.

Dad had said he was sick and tired of the whole rock star gig. But when I saw him onstage I knew that he could never give it up. He was the real deal. The guy couldn't live without his music and probably all the frills, like Daisy, that came with it.

"You'd disappoint your fans if you didn't speak with them," I said, my words dripping with attitude.

"Hey, watch the sassy mouth!" he said.

I felt like shooting back another sarcastic comment but knew better. I just stared straight ahead.

"So who was that on the phone?"

"Tammy! She invited me to Wisconsin for a few days. Can I go?"

We'd been walking on a city street and he stopped now to look at me. "You're not having a good time?" he asked.

"It's fine. It's just… Tammy is at this big air show in Wisconsin and we've hardly seen each other all summer. And it's so close to here. I could meet you in a few days in Cleveland." I looked down at the ground. The truth was that I wasn't having such a good time. It was not at all like I'd expected and I felt like I hardly knew this person who was standing next to me.

"You mean the Experimental Aircraft Association Fly-in?" he said.

I was surprised he knew about it, but then again, he had grown up in Indiana.

"Yeah. That's the one!"

"I played there once. A long time ago, before I got my big break. The Fly-In's a gas," he said quietly.

I searched his face. "You mean, it's okay for me to go?" I asked feeling conflicted. I was excited but felt bad at the same time.

"As long as you promise to be a good girl," he said in his most fatherly way, but it sounded silly to me.

"I'm always a good girl," I said, trying to suppress my annoyance. This just felt so wrong. I was confused. Up until I was 12, I had spent most of my time dreaming about finding my dad. And now that I had found him, I realized he wasn't the person I had expected. He'd never be like other dads. He was David Peer, the rock star!

"Oshkosh's only about three hours away, so I'll call a car for you," he said.

"Thanks," I said, grateful that I'd be getting a break from it all. "I have to tell Tammy! She'll be so excited," I said and started texting her.

"**Yay!**" was her immediate response.

I smiled at this stranger who was my father.

"I know you're only going away for a few days, but I'm going to miss you," he said sweetly. I fought back tears. Was I making a mistake? I couldn't believe I was leaving him now.

I started feeling nervous all of a sudden. When I think about it now, I realize that was when it started. It was at that moment, that very moment when I got those second thoughts about leaving my dad.

That's when the ringing in my ears began.

CHAPTER THREE

Ear Training

"So don't forget to call," said Dad, trying his best to sound father-like again. It was the next morning. We stood in the downstairs hotel lobby, both packed and ready to go.

"See you on Saturday," I said coolly. He bent over to hug me and I responded woodenly. I just needed some space, I told myself. I could tell he was hurt, but I figured he'd get over it. He was a big boy.

I needed some time to think about things. It would be great to be at the air show with Tammy for five whole days. Moments later, I found myself in a limo heading to Oshkosh, Wisconsin.

I sank back into the plush leather seat and started flipping through channels on the TV set. Having a rock star dad did have its perks—I got to ride in limos.

The first time I'd ridden in one had been three years before, when I'd won tickets to one of my dad's concerts. He didn't even know I existed back then. That day turned out to be a disaster. I never saw the concert, never spoke to Dad, and didn't ride home in the limo. His people thought I was a kook when I said I was his daughter. They threw me out.

Like I said, it was a total disaster. But it all worked out in the end. Thank God.

I pushed the remote. *The Nanny* came on. I loved that show even if it was ancient. But I'd seen that episode many times and nothing else on TV grabbed me. I turned it off and gazed out my window at cows and green pastures yawning in either direction. I wouldn't be in Oshkosh until lunchtime. Feeling restless, I raided the mini fridge. Grabbing a granola bar, I thought about the piano.

I had been practicing a lot on the tour. So why not work on my piano playing now? After all, a glass pane separated me from the driver, so the backseat could be my own private practice room. I pulled out my mini Yamaha keyboard from my backpack, recalling that we had run into Dad's keyboard player Randy Macy after dinner the night before.

"We just went to TJs!" Dad told the gangly Englishman as he stepped into the hotel elevator right after us. "We heard a great blues band." I think both of us were grateful to have someone else there.

"Brilliant!" said Randy. Dad met Randy at a rock festival in London a few years before, and they'd worked together ever since.

"Are you in the mood to play some blues, Zoey?" Randy asked, grinning at me.

"Okay," I said. The three of us went to Dad's room and played some standard blues tunes like "Hoochie Coochie Man" for about an hour. Randy and I shared the keyboard and Dad played guitar. That was what I loved most about touring with Dad. Someone was always making music, day or night.

"She sounds good, David," said Randy after I played a heady solo in F. They both clapped.

"I think Zoey should sit in on our next show!"

Dad beamed with pride. "That's a great idea!"

"Thanks, but I think I have to wash my hair that night," I said. This wasn't the first time they'd said that. It was kind of a running joke with us. I knew I wasn't ready to perform at a concert. I didn't want to get on stage just because I was David Peer's kid. I wanted to be great. I wanted to play my own songs.

I'm not in any rush, I thought as I sat in the limo, rifling through my backpack for my iPod.

I knew I had a lot to learn, which is why I wanted to take some time during the limo ride to practice ear training.

The first time I'd ever heard of ear training or really understood what ear training meant was when singer Kim Doucette got booked to appear in one of Dad's shows. Her manager called a day before the show and said she wanted to sing her hit "Hologram" with Dad and the band. Me, I would have needed sheet music, but not these guys.

They just listened to the CD, sat down and started winging it. No one told them what key it was in or what notes to play. By the time Kim arrived the next day for a run-through, they sounded like they'd been playing that song for years!

That's because they'd all had ear training. They had learned how to identify notes just by hearing them. I wanted to do that. So one day, when Dad was giving some press interviews and I had nothing to do, Randy decided to give me a lesson.

"Get comfortable," he said to me as we sat in the trailer. It was parked right outside the Atlanta Civic Auditorium. Everyone else had gone to lunch.

He closed the windows to make the trailer quiet. "Now focus on the music I'm about to play without any distractions. Block out all extraneous noises. Forget about the air conditioner and the refrigerator and the hum of the toilet."

I had to chuckle about that. That toilet had a life of its own. It gurgled all day and got backed up at the worst moments.

"Don't get too relaxed! I want you to be comfortable but alert. I want you to listen and listen carefully," he said, pressing the button on the audio system. My father's hit tune "Castles" filled the trailer.

"With lots of practice, this will become second nature," he assured me. I focused on the song. I loved "Castles" but I wasn't listening to it for enjoyment that day.

"Try to find the melody line. Let the song get inside your brain. You have to become one with the music," Randy said.

After a few more times, he turned off the music and was ready to test my tonal memory. I tried to play the melody on my keyboard, using only my right hand. I got a few notes into it and then got stuck.

"Errrrrrrrr," I groaned. He restarted the song and we repeated the process again and again. By the end of my "lesson" I was playing "Castles" smoothly with both hands!

I had made pretty good progress since that day and now it was time to get back to work, I thought as I loaded my iPod into the dock in the back of the limo. It was time to listen. I put the iPod on shuffle, waiting for the device to randomly select a song.

"Runaway Train" by Soul Asylum came on. I listened, trying to figure out where one phrase ended and another began. I picked out the verses, the bridge and then the chorus.

After a few listens, I tried to play it on my keyboard. And after several attempts, I figured out "Runaway Train."

It was definitely getting easier. I then moved on to "Clocks" by Coldplay. Three hours passed before I knew it. I had completely lost myself in the music. The next song that came up was "American Pie" by Don McLean. Great song.

"This is about the day the music died," Mom told me one day as she drove me to school. The song had just come on the radio. "People call it that because three huge stars, Ritchie Valens, Buddy Holly and the Big Bopper, all died in a plane crash in Iowa."

Mom may not have been as musical as Dad or I, but she knew more stuff about music history than both of us combined. A lot of people knew about "The Day the Music Died," but Mom could tell you all about the concert that the three guys were playing in before they got on that plane. She taught a course about rock music and its impact on history at Harlan University.

"American Pie" was an amazing song, but it was over eight minutes long. There's no way I could ever ear train on that, I thought. Suddenly, I felt a cold shiver.

Why had this song about a plane crash in the Midwest come on just as I was heading to an air show in that part of the country? Weird.

I tried to ignore a growing feeling of uneasiness as I listened to the song, gearing myself up to play it when the limo driver spoke for the first time in hours.

"We're almost there. We should be meeting your friend in about ten minutes," he said through a mike. Tammy and I had arranged to meet at a gas station on a country road about two miles from the air show. I could see the station coming up.

I quickly put away my keyboard and leaned over to shut off the iPod, but noticed something strange. The iPod had already been turned off.

But "American Pie" was still playing loud and clear in my ears. What? I shook my head a few times to clear it. It was no use. I couldn't get rid of the music. I'd had songs stuck in my mind before, but this was different. Don McLean's voice rang right through me as if I were an iPod and the song was an MP3 file downloaded to my brain. Looking back, I know that this was the moment when I started morphing into ear training.

The whole matter lasted only thirty seconds and was quickly forgotten in the next moment when I looked up and saw my best friend's smiling face through the window.

"Hi!" I screeched, waving to Tammy. The song and all thoughts of it disappeared from my head until the next day when those very same chords mysteriously materialized in my ears during Nathan's disappearing act.

CHAPTER FOUR

Air Training

I stepped out of the car and straight into Tammy's bouncing embrace. We were both jumping up and down with excitement.

"There's a barbecue by the lake," said Tammy, her green eyes sparkling brightly, picking up the lush green grass surrounding us. Her eyes were striking against her red hair, which had earned her a lot of teasing in her youth. But now it was "Carrot Top" Tammy who was having the last laugh because she was drop-dead gorgeous.

And the most beautiful thing about her was that she didn't know it. Or at least, she didn't let on that she knew it.

She was still the same old zany Tammy I'd known since preschool. Both our moms worked at Harlan University. We'd gone to childcare and preschool and after-school care together. I think Tammy knew me better than anyone. And she could say the same about me.

After we finished our little happy dance, Tammy pulled my luggage from the limo and put it in her dad's rental car. I took a moment to feel the warm sun on my face, to smell the fresh country air. I'd been living in and out of suitcases for weeks, shuttling between buses, planes and trains all around Atlanta, New York and Chicago. Each city had been amazing, but big and overwhelming as well. It seemed so calm and quiet here in comparison. For now, anyway.

"Nice set of wheels Zoey!" said Tammy's dad, Dan, from their car's driver seat. I waved at the limo driver as he turned the car around and headed back to Chicago.

"What would you expect? She's a celeb now!" said Tammy as we got in the backseat.

"Oh, cut it out," I said defensively.

"Okay. Sorry," said Tammy.

I hated it when she pulled that celebrity stuff. She'd been there three years ago when the news hit and the press had gone wild. Troubled rocker nearly dies, gets amnesia, lives hard on the road, finds fame and then meets long-lost love child after 12 years.

No one can ever be prepared for a media blitz, especially when it's about your own life. I'd so much rather be anonymous. It had finally calmed down a little, thank goodness. I hoped the press continued to focus on things besides my relationship with my dad.

"Okay," I said shooting her a "don't you dare treat me any different" look.

Tammy nodded apologetically. "But how's it been? How's your dad?" she asked with concern.

"It's been nice," I said, missing him all of a sudden.

"Great. I've got to introduce you to some really cool people," said Tammy, probably sensing she needed to change the subject.

"I want you to meet my friend Ruby. You've never met anyone like her. She loves to fly. She lives to fly! This week, she's gotten hooked on a weird little ultra-light aircraft," she said.

I smiled at Tammy as she blabbered on and on about this girl, Ruby, but inside I felt funny all of a sudden. I couldn't put my finger on it and I certainly didn't want to ruin the moment for Tammy. Maybe I felt bad about leaving dad, I thought.

"So now she's hoping to get a vendor's license for it," Tammy said as we approached the east end of the air show grounds.

And what a sight it was. It was like nothing I'd seen. Row after row after row of small planes were parked in the endless country fields. Tents were pitched beneath the planes. I immediately forgot my worries.

We drove past the campgrounds towards the cookout.

"Come on, let's go," said Tammy when we got there. The barbecue was on a grassy field by a lake. Boats were tethered to docks along the shore. But when I looked at them again, I realized they were not boats. They were seaplanes.

One came in for a landing on the lake right as we stood there. It landed with a huge splash. Water sprayed on people standing nearby, but no one seemed to mind. They laughed and clapped.

The plane taxied slowly on the water towards a slip. I noticed Tammy's mom, Leeza, a few feet away, talking to some people by a grill. She smiled at us and walked over and gave me a hug.

"How's life in the rock and roll lane?" she asked, smiling.

Leeza would be calling my mom to give her an update faster than I could say Oshkosh, so I kept it upbeat, smiling and gave her a thumbs-up.

"It's great," I said.

"How's your dad?"

"Good. He played here once," I said noticing a four-piece band setting up under a tree across the lawn.

"I wish he was playing this year! I can't wait to meet him already," said Leeza.

"He'll be staying with us in the fall. You'll meet him then," I said. Tammy yanked on my sweatshirt sleeve.

"There she is! There's Ruby, the girl I told you about!" She pointed through the crowd to a tomboyish-looking girl with short dark brown hair who was laughing with a slender blonde guy.

"And that's Nathan. He's a pilot and works for upMobile, the company that makes the paraplane. He does a lot of things, actually." Nathan wasn't much taller than Ruby and she seemed petite. It was hard to tell their age, but they both looked young.

"How old are they?" I asked.

"They're about twenty-four. I'm the baby in the group," she said, taking my hand. "See you later mom. We're going to say hi to Ruby." Tammy pulled me like a puppy towards her new friends. Why was Tammy so obsessed with these people?

"Hey!" I said stopping dead in my tracks and making her trip backwards.

"What are you doing?" she said annoyed, but then saw my face and shut up.

"Why are you so gaga over these people? Have you gone flying with them or something?" Actually, that was exactly the kind of thing Tammy would do. She was fearless and would do almost anything, at least once. I think it was because her dad was a pilot, so Tammy had flying in her blood. But he said she couldn't take flying lessons until she maintained a B average. And she hadn't, which is why I was so suspicious.

Tammy rolled her eyes but looked over her shoulder nervously. "Are you crazy? I'm not that stupid!" she said.

She was definitely not stupid, but sometimes a little reckless. Over the years, Tammy had gotten me into some pretty wild situations.

"I just don't get this fixation with Ruby all of a sudden," I said. Maybe I was a little jealous too. After all, I'd left my dad's tour just to see her. And here she was having a girl crush on Ruby.

"You'll see. It's the flying," said Tammy. "She's just so excited about flying. It kind of reminds me of …you. The way you are about your music," she said.

"Fine," I rolled my eyes and let her drag me towards Ruby the Wonder Woman.

"Hey Tammy," said Ruby, smiling. She and her boyfriend Nathan seemed friendly enough.

"Hi Zoey," said Nathan, extending his hand to shake mine.

"Welcome to Oshkosh!" said Ruby. "I can't believe I'm meeting the daughter of David Peer. Wow."

Wow was right. I should just switch my name to David Peer's Daughter, I thought, since it seemed that no one would ever be interested in Zoey Browne again.

"Oops," said Tammy, turning to Ruby. "I probably should have waited for Zoey to tell you about her dad. I just got so excited!"

"Don't worry. We won't tell a soul," said Nathan earnestly and then leaned towards Ruby. "Although, we could write it in the sky."

Ruby fought a smile. I grinned, feeling a little stupid. "Tammy tells me you guys do a lot of flying," I said.

"Ruby never flew a day in her life until she met Nathan at this show three years ago. And now flying's her whole life," Tammy explained to me. Ruby nodded, her eyes dancing.

"I had barely travelled outside of Wisconsin," she said squeezing Nathan's hand. "But I got curious about this show so I decided to check it out. And every year, something wonderful happens here! This year, I walked by a booth and saw a sign that said 'Learn to Fly in 60 Minutes' that caught my eye!" she said.

My jaw dropped. I'd never had flight training, but I knew you couldn't learn to fly in 60 minutes. These people were crazy!

Ruby, Tammy and Nathan all exchanged mysterious glances, which gave me a funny feeling.

Just then a voice boomed over a loudspeaker. "Attention ladies and gentlemen. The Blue Angels will be giving the last air show of the day at 4:30! Get down to the Flight Line and grab a lawn chair. You don't want to miss this show, just east of the Fly Market and Amelia's Eatery. It will be spectacular! And then tomorrow morning, we have a really special treat with the world premiere of Cougar Aviation's latest twin engine model, the Silo! Don't miss the demo at 10 am sharp!"

Nathan flipped out. "The Silo! I've been hearing about that new plane for a while. It's a canard-winged turboprop. We have to check it out!" he said to Ruby.

"Isn't that the plane Cougar's been working on for years?" she asked.

He nodded. "Nobody but Lake Aircraft has ever put anything like that on the market. And Lake only put it into limited production," Nathan said.

"I read that there had been a lot of complications," Ruby said. "They've postponed it many times." But Nathan was already onto something else.

"So Zoey," he said. "Want to see how you can fly in 60 minutes?"

My stomach churned. And were it not for the sounds of the splashing seaplanes and the chattering people, I would've detected the soft timbre rising up in my ears. But I didn't hear it yet. All I noticed was a little itching in my ears, and that could've been from anything.

CHAPTER FIVE

Up and Up

My concern about the paraplane turned out to be unfounded. A little while later, I stood waving up to Ruby as she swooped above us in the funny-looking contraption. It was basically a motorized lawn chair dangling from a parachute. Ruby's smile was radiant even from an altitude of 500 feet above the cornfields.

"You're right," I said to Tammy. "There is something really special about her."

"I knew you'd like her," said Tammy. "That paraplane's cool, too, isn't it?"

I nodded. I guess it was pretty safe since it used a parachute, but it was nothing I'd want to go up in. I'd done enough unconventional flying through my musi-morphing.

I looked at Tammy, though, and wondered how long I'd be able to keep her feet on the ground. Maybe Tammy's dad would be okay with the paraplane if he checked it out with her first. But knowing Tammy, I doubted she'd consider seeking her father's opinion.

"You've got to fly this!" Ruby exclaimed as she glided gracefully into a landing right near us. I had a flash of

Amelia Earhart for a second. We had read about her in Social Studies last year. I looked at this girl, this aviatress and wondered if she could musi-morph. Was she musical as well? I felt like I had met Ruby somewhere.

"Do you play an instrument?" I asked her as we walked back to the campsite. She gave Nathan a quick glance before answering.

"Flute," she said.

Nathan jerked his head in surprise. "Ruby! You've never told me you played the flute!" he smiled. "I played the clarinet in high school," he said proudly.

Now it was Ruby's turn to be surprised.

"You guys should try playing together," I said.

"I haven't picked it up in years," she said with a faraway look in her eyes. "Who has time between work and flying?"

We were back by their tent. Nathan put his arm around her. "Well, I'm glad you like flying," he said, cupping a hand over his eyes to stare up at a formation of military planes flying overhead. "Those are great looking Flying Fortresses. I'd love to get my hands on one of them," he said.

We all squinted into the sunshine to watch the planes.

"Is there anything you wouldn't fly?" asked Ruby, lightly kissing him on the cheek.

"Probably not. I don't think there's a plane in this whole airfield I wouldn't take up at least once!" he said.

"Crazy pilots," said Ruby, hugging him.

Just then, a white-haired 50-ish looking man in a polo shirt and jeans approached the campsite. Nathan stood up a little straighter.

The man came over to shake Nathan's hand. "Nathan Gordon? I'm John Kiefer, CEO of Cougar. How do you do?"

"Nice to meet you, Mr. Kiefer. I've always been a big fan of Cougar. To what do I owe this pleasure?" asked Nathan. I could tell he was wondering why this bigwig would turn up at his campsite knowing his name.

"We should go," I murmured, sensing the guy wanted to talk business.

"I'll walk you guys over to your campsite," said Ruby.

We said quick goodbyes to Nathan and John Kiefer and headed to our tent, which was across the big field.

"You know, Zoey, it's interesting that you brought up music," said Ruby.

I looked at her curiously.

"A few years ago my life was a mess. Then I found flying and Nathan. It changed everything," she said wistfully.

"Why was your life a mess?" Tammy asked softly.

"I had a very serious boyfriend. We were both musicians but we had a bad breakup. He went to Germany and I never heard from him again. I gave up the flute after that. I couldn't even look at it," she said.

"Maybe you should pick it up again," I said. Again, I had the strangest feeling that I'd met her somewhere, sometime before. Or was it that we were destined to meet somewhere and sometime in another alternative and magical musical universe? Tammy was right. There was definitely something very special about Ruby Lewis.

And it had to do with Musicland.

CHAPTER SIX

Out of Thin Air

I t turns out Kiefer wanted Nathan to fly the Silo in the air show demo the following day.

"Cougar needed someone in a pinch to demonstrate that new Silo, and some big finance guy named Tony Zapallero recommended Nathan. They're paying him five thousand dollars," Ruby told us as she stepped out of her tent the next morning. Nathan had already left.

"Five thousand dollars?" I couldn't believe my ears. That was a lot of money. "Does Nathan normally make that much for something like this?" I asked.

"No," she said quietly. "They went over to Cougar Aviation headquarters last night for hours to go over some things," she adding. She did not seem very excited about the whole idea.

"What happened to the original pilot?" asked Tammy.

"Family emergency," said Ruby. "Nathan's really excited, though, and said he'd buy us all dinner." But she sounded gloomy. My ears itched, but I shrugged it off as allergies.

Something was making me nervous again.

"You want to go to the Silo's hangar with me?" Ruby asked, sounding chirpier. "Nathan's doing a final pre-flight inspection."

"Sure," Tammy and I said in unison. We walked to the hangar where the Silo was parked and found Kiefer and Nathan there.

"You're not planning on taking anyone up, are you?" Kiefer said to Nathan as soon as we walked in.

"Of course not!" said Nathan with a laugh.

Kiefer smiled. "I'm just making sure. Cougar has strict rules about these things," he said. For some reason, I just didn't trust this guy.

"Got it," said Nathan. "Ruby and these young ladies are just my little cheering section," he said, smiling at us as he walked around, inspecting the Silo. Ruby followed closely on his heels.

"Sounds great." Kiefer checked his watch. "You're good to go then. Thank you again for piloting our plane's virgin flight." He handed Nathan an envelope.

Nathan looked inside and saw wads of hundred dollar bills. He laughed. "Aren't you supposed to pay me after the flight?"

Kiefer smiled like a Cheshire cat. "We've decided that we're so grateful to you for helping us on such short notice that we're going to give you a bonus stock option package after the flight."

Nathan whistled appreciatively. "That is very nice indeed. Thank you Mr. Kiefer," he said.

"My pleasure," Kiefer said nodding. "I'm going to leave you now to your cheering section so I can get a good seat for the show. Good luck!"

We watched him walk away. He definitely gave me the creeps.

"Wow!" Nathan peeked into the envelope again before handing it to Ruby."Don't spend it all one place!" he said.

"Just get down in one piece!" said Ruby as she stuffed the envelope in her jeans pocket.

"Don't worry baby. We'll be dining in grand style before you know it. Help me check everything," he said and began walking around the plane again with Ruby.

After they were done, Nathan looked at his watch. "It's time," he said and swept Ruby dramatically in his arms, kissing her long and hard on the lips. "I love you," he whispered.

"I love you too," she said, fighting back tears.

"Good luck Nathan!" Tammy said cheerfully. "Come on, Ruby. Let's get seats," she said guiding Ruby gently out of the hangar.

After we found a spot in the bleachers, I noticed John Kiefer sitting a few feet away. He got up to talk to another guy in a row ahead of us who looked more mobster than pilot in his expensive Italian suit and fancy leather shoes.

"That's Zapallero, the finance guy who had recommended Nathan for the job," whispered Ruby, pointing at him. A bored-looking blonde bombshell sat next to him. On the other side of the girl was a cute guy with blonde hair and green eyes. He turned around and smiled at me. My heart fluttered.

"I'm glad it worked out with Gordon," the mobster said to Kiefer, but the rest of the conversation was drowned out by the C note that started blasting in my ear as Nathan took off in the Silo. I forgot about the cute guy and everything else.

For that's when the nightmare began. One minute, Nathan was there, the next minute he was gone.

CHAPTER SEVEN

Night Song

Hours after the Silo disaster, we convinced Ruby to lie down. We had talked to dozens of policemen and aviation officials. Nobody knew what to make of it. The press was already swarming so we snuck Ruby to our tent to give her some peace.

There wasn't much else we could do. Tammy looked like she had been hit by a truck. Her eyes were swollen and red. I was looking at her, wondering if either of us would ever be the same, when I realized I had left my backpack at the hangar where we'd last seen Nathan that morning. It felt like a week ago.

"I have to go back to the hangar," I told Tammy.

"Do you want me to come with you?" she offered.

"No," I said, shaking my head. "You should get some sleep. I'll meet you back here." She nodded, grateful to be off the hook. We came together in a fierce hug. Neither of us could express the way we felt, but we knew we were in for a crazy scary ride of sorts. Tammy and I had been through a lot together, but this was beyond bizarre.

I started walking across the field towards the hangar when the chords came back with great force. I felt as if I was moving in a sort of musical trance.

My ears tingled and the chords began to change in quicker succession. I started to recognize a pattern – they were forming the progression of "American Pie"!

When I got to the hangar, it was dark and empty and kind of creepy. I felt like running away but I couldn't. The strangest thing was happening. I was getting an intensely strong urge to play my keyboard right then, right there. It was as if the chords in my mind were commanding me to play.

I turned on the light and stared at the empty space where the Silo had been and a profound sadness washed over me. I shoved these feelings aside as I heard the chords again. I saw my backpack, stashed in the corner where I had left it hours ago. I walked over and unzipped it and was relieved to find my Yamaha. I pulled it out. It felt weird to be playing it out here, but I couldn't stop myself if I tried. I sat cross-legged on the floor right there and I started it up. I hit a key, and the sound clashed with the notes in my head. I pounded my thigh in frustration. What was I doing? I felt tears well up in eyes.

I cursed the instrument. I cursed the air show. I cursed Cougar and Kiefer. But then my fingers went back to the keys and I tried the opening riff of "American Pie."

This time, something different happened. It actually sounded good. It was as if I had been playing the song for months. I remembered all the tricks that Randy had showed me regarding ear training. The music flowed straight from my heart through my hands and onto the keys. I kept playing, and the song filled the hangar.

And then it happened. I was morphing. The musical element I was studying, ear training, had overtaken my body. I felt the hangar shake. I knew exactly what was going on. The first time this had happened, three years before, was in a practice room at the university where Mom worked. I had been terrified. I had been locked inside that practice room with no way out. The music had flowed from my heart through my hands onto the piano and soon the entire room had begun to shake. Then it had completely wiggled free of its foundation and lifted, taking me away from this world to another one far, far away through distant and exotic skies.

That was the first time I realized the correlation between my playing and a room's movement. Now as it started to happen again, I felt a peaceful calm. I knew this wasn't an earthquake even as I felt another sharp jolt. I knew my music was making the hangar move so violently.

I played harder, and the building started prying itself free from the ground. It had been three years since I'd musi-morphed, but it felt like it was yesterday. I was heading to a musical world that revealed life's truths in beautiful but sometimes mysterious and dangerous ways.

My hands moved faster and harder and then with one final, big jolt, the hangar broke loose from the ground and started to lift.

I kept playing "American Pie." Soon I was sailing through a night sky filled with violins, music stands, pianos, clarinets and other musical objects. Then the landscape changed and I was gliding through a cartoon-like panorama of lavender and purple mountains.

How could I have missed the signs over the last few days? Now there was no denying why I'd been hearing those chords. The music had come to me for a reason. It was bringing me back to Musicland for a purpose. And it had to do with the terrible thing that had happened to Nathan. I was certain of that.

The hangar came to a gentle stop with a soft little swoosh. I peeked outside. The building appeared to be perched on a tree overlooking a small wooded area.

Where had I landed? Musicland changed each time I got there. What year was it? I didn't know yet, but I knew I would find out soon.

I stepped out of the hangar into a grassy meadow. My hands twitched with the music still pulsing through them. The bushes and the foliage were an interesting otherworldly contrast of hot pink and dark turquoise. The turquoise reminded me of a cold Midwestern lake where a pilot may easily go missing and I was again reminded sadly of Nathan. And then my mind jumped to Buddy Holly, Ritchie Valens and the Big Bopper and the Day the Music Died.

Was there a connection somehow? Is that why I had morphed playing "American Pie," the song Don McLean had dedicated to those musicians? He had coined the phrase "The Day the Music Died" in his song.

That phrase had become synonymous with the day those three legendary rockers died in Clear Lake, Iowa, a Midwestern town just a few hours from where Nathan disappeared.

That song, "American Pie," had been running through my mind for days. It had popped into my head on my way to Oshkosh and then again when Nathan disappeared. Something was going on.

I heard the sound of rustling bushes and turned around. I saw an image that would've terrified a normal person. But I had long ago given up hope that my life would ever be normal. And so I was ecstatic rather than horrified by the sight in front of me. It was Amadeus, a purple talking squirrel.

Of course the first time I'd met him here in Musicland I nearly fainted. But I'd gotten used to Amadeus and other talking animals around here. Many of these creatures possess human-like qualities, great musical talent in particular.

Wherever you wound up, whether it was Woodstock in the 1960s or the deck of the Titanic in 1912, you saw these musical creatures side-by-side with humans.

"You've grown!" Amadeus said in his nasally British accent.

I smiled, fighting the urge to rush up and hug him. I knew he'd freak out and just scurry away like a regular squirrel would.

"How are you doing, Amadeus?"

Ignoring my question, he asked another. "How old are you now, fifteen?"

I nodded. Amadeus had greeted me at this landing spot the very first time I had arrived here. And he'd been my welcoming committee ever since.

"Imagine being fifteen and going to the last performance of some of the greatest musicians who have ever lived," said the squirrel, now assuming his teacher-like stance.

I knew immediately where he was heading with this. "Is it 1959?" I asked. Mom had taught a class about the Day the Music Died. That's why I knew the date.

"Bingo! It's 1959 and you're in Clear Lake, Iowa on the day of Winter Dance Party show at the Surf Ballroom," the squirrel said, confirming my thoughts.

"I knew it!" I gasped. I had travelled to Buddy Holly's last show.

"Let's go! There's no time for chit-chat. Timing is everything with both flight and music. You will soon see that these two passions have much in common. Understanding this connection will help on this very important journey to Musicland," he said, and began racing down a wooded path.

I scrambled to keep up with him as the song again played loudly in my brain. "What about the connection between flight and music? I saw a pilot disappear in flight." I said, catching my breath as I caught up with him.

Now I heard more music, but this time it was not coming from inside my head. It was from somewhere around here in these woods. It was Buddy Holly's hit "Peggy Sue."

"Step it up!" demanded Amadeus. "I am not the expert on the subject, but clearly both pilots and musicians rely on their instincts in real time to make split second decisions that affect how things come out," he said.

I nodded. This was true.

"Sadly, the two passions have often intersected in tragedy. The world has lost some of its greatest musicians to air disasters," he said. "You clearly know about Buddy Holly, Ritchie Valens and the Big Bopper. But the list goes on and on," he said.

"Many famous singers and musicians have been lost in the skies. Patsy Cline, John Denver, members of the Lynyrd Skynyrd band, Aaliyah, Glenn Miller just to name a few," said Amadeus, adding, "Otis Redding and Stevie Ray Vaughan also died in air crashes in Wisconsin."

I shivered as I thought about all the musicians who'd gone down in planes. I'd always loved the blues. Stevie Ray Vaughan had been a particular favorite of mine and my dad's. Dad said it was one of the saddest days of his life when he learned that Stevie Ray Vaughan had died in a helicopter crash in Wisconsin after playing in a concert with Eric Clapton and Robert Cray. Dad said he'd spent months perfecting his own blues and learned every Stevie Ray riff he could get his hands on. Much of his music was inspired by the late, great bluesman.

And Mom had told me about the R&B singer Otis Redding who'd died in a plane crash in Wisconsin just days after he recorded his hit, "(Sittin' On) The Dock of the Bay." He never got to see the song climb the charts and become the mega hit it was. I felt myself shiver with these thoughts.

But I also shivered because it was really cold outside in Iowa in February. Seemingly out of nowhere, Amadeus produced a parka and tossed it back to me. I hastily put it on and felt warmer.

"It was freezing that night in Iowa in February 1959. Holly was tired of riding the bus because its heating system kept breaking down. It was so cold on that bus, in fact, that one of the band members got frostbite," he said.

I followed him, listening to the Holly classic through the strikingly colored woods and felt the urge to play it myself.

"You know how the story ends, don't you?" he asked.

"Yes. Buddy Holly decided to charter a plane for himself and his friends," I said. Amadeus stopped abruptly and I almost trampled him. I looked over to where he was staring. There it was: The Surf Ballroom.

Inside, the show was in full swing as Texas DJ Giles P. Richardson, better known as the Big Bopper, rocked the house with his glorious hit, "Chantilly Lace."

The hypnotic chorus spread all through the woods to us. I heard the crowd inside screaming with joy.

"That's the Big Bopper," I said.

"Yes. That's right," said Amadeus, smiling in that funky squirrel way of his.

I smiled too, but there really wasn't anything to smile about. We were there hearing the last show of some of music history's greatest spirits, just hours before they'd perish. I started to tear up.

"Don't get upset now Zoey. Think how lucky you are to be here to hear this. I thought we'd pop into the show for a second, so you can see it, hear it and feel it," Amadeus said.

It was true. I was fortunate to be in Musicland, where the past and the present blended together musically. I was lucky to be there to experience the last show by three of the world's best loved rock 'n' rollers. The crash had happened shortly after the plane took off. It didn't get far from the airport before it went down, killing all on board.

I read about it when my mom was putting it into one of her lectures at Harlan University. There had been a heavy snowfall that night in February 1959. The pilot was inexperienced with instrument navigation, which is what he had to rely on because he couldn't see very much outside due to the bad weather.

The wing hit the ground and the small plane corkscrewed over and over. The three young artists were thrown clear out of the plane.

I tried to shake these images out of my head as I approached the Surf Ballroom. It got easier as I got swept up into the excitement and the music.

The place was so alive. A crowd of people and those human-like animals were gathered outside the building. They hadn't been lucky enough to score tickets but wanted to be part of the scene anyway.

I was reminded of Oshkosh, where just a few hours earlier, I had been at another big Midwestern gathering. I thought of Nathan and suddenly had the distinct feeling that he was there.

CHAPTER EIGHT

Surf Ballroom

We made our way through the crowd and Amadeus waved two tickets to a big man guarding the entrance. The mob inside was even more revved up than the group outside.

The ballroom was decorated with a surf motif, thus its title. Murals of huge splashing waves covered the walls and faux palm trees were planted on stage. The infectiously upbeat song, "Chantilly Lace" reverberated off the walls as the Big Bopper shook, rattled and rolled on stage.

I looked through the crowd for Nathan. Again, I felt I sensed him. Could he really be there? Was that why I was there?

"Do you think my friend is here?" I shouted to Amadeus over the music.

"Yes," he said.

I turned around to face him head on. "He's here? Please take me to him!" I half-screamed, trying to contain myself.

Amadeus shook his head. "I wish I could, but I can't. I don't know where he is exactly, but I do know that you need to stop him from getting on that plane!"

My heart started beating fast. "What plane? What do you mean I need to stop him?" I asked, but I had a terrible feeling I knew which plane he meant.

"Buddy Holly's plane!" exclaimed Amadeus. "The manager of the Surf Ballroom was asked by Buddy Holly's people to find a pilot and that was just about the time Nathan arrived."

"Arrived?" I stammered.

"He musi-morphed here. He wound up backstage with the crew as they were setting up the stage. And then he heard about the flight and volunteered for the job," said Amadeus.

He sounded calm but I detected an edge in his voice. "Your friend did not musi-morph himself here. Someone else sent him here and wants him to fly in that....disastrous mission," said the squirrel, now sounding more frantic than me.

"What are you saying? Is someone trying to murder him here in Musicland? And how can I stop it?" I asked, feeling my knees get all wobbly.

Could this really be happening? My mind played over the last scene in that hangar with John Kiefer. What had he said? Had he left any clues? I liked that guy less and less with each minute and I had the feeling he had something to do with Nathan's vanishing.

"I'm not sure, Zoey. But I told you that you'd be learning more about the relationship between flight and music as you embark on this journey. Well, here's your first big lesson. You must save your friend. You're the only who can do it!"

I stared speechlessly at him as the music grew louder again. Ritchie Valens was crooning his unforgettable tune, "La Bamba," and the crowd was going wild.

He finished to loud applause and enthusiastic cheering. After calming down a bit, the audience grew frenzied again as a nerdy looking guy with thick glasses took to the stage. There he was, Buddy Holly. The rock icon adored around the world whose fame had grown even more enormous after his tragic death.

Holly had led the way for many great musicians. John Lennon idolized him and even named the Beatles as a nod to Holly's group, the Crickets.

I watched Holly strut the stage, playing his guitar and singing with ferocious energy. His thick glasses had become his trademark and spawned a trend once he embraced them. He had tried to perform without them but his eyesight was poor. As his fame grew, young people everywhere began wearing those glasses.

Dad's friend Rodney, who taught him everything he knew on guitar, had seen Buddy Holly in Ohio just a few weeks before his final Surf Ballroom show.

I could see why so many people loved him. Hearing him live was incredible, even though this was all a replica of a real show in another world. Holly kept playing and playing and playing. After he took his bows, he came back for a whole second set. The place rocked. I felt myself getting lost in the music, forgetting for a while that I was there to save Nathan.

Suddenly the horrible memory of his disappearance came back to me and I remembered what Amadeus had said. I was the only one who could save him. I couldn't understand that.

How could I keep him from getting on that plane? Could he really die here in Musicland? I knew I had come close once myself. I had to try to find the manager of the Surf Ballroom who'd hired Nathan to fly the plane. If Nathan did get on that plane, he may really be gone for good.

I turned around to look for Amadeus but he was nowhere to be found. I hated when he did that to me. I scanned the crowd for Nathan. I didn't see anyone who looked familiar at all. I moved through the crowd, still rocking to the music, and saw an exit. I had to find the manager of the Surf Ballroom, and fast. Nathan's life depended on it.

I stepped into the main lobby. There was a snack concession that had been abandoned. Everyone was watching the show. I walked up to the bouncer who was guarding the door.

"Excuse me. Do you know where the manager is? I have to talk with him urgently," I said.

"He's probably watching the show, but his office is down that hall. His name is Max Barnes," said the guy, who was built like a quarterback. He pointed to a corridor right off the lobby.

"Thanks," I said, walking down the hall. The music blared from the ballroom but it was a little quieter out there and I tried to clear my head. I had to think fast. I walked to a door that said "Manager" on it and knocked. Nobody answered.

I looked around nervously. Nobody was nearby so I turned the knob and let myself in. There were many posters on the walls from past concerts and a big pile of papers on the desk.

I wasn't looking for anything in particular. I didn't want to get in trouble. I just had to stop this guy from putting Nathan on the plane.

Just then I heard footsteps coming down the hall and froze. Soon, a moose standing on two legs came rushing into the room and stopped dead in his tracks when he saw me.

"Who the heck are you and what are you doing in my office?" he asked. Despite his angry tone, he seemed like a gentle spirited moose.

I'd soon find out that Max Barnes wasn't really a great concert hall manager. He had a tough time keeping track of details and logistics. But he loved music so much he wouldn't have given up his job for anything. He loved being able to say he got to hang with musicians like the great Buddy Holly.

"Hi. I'm here from...Wisconsin. I'm looking for my brother. He escaped a mental institute," I said, trying to sound convincing. I had concocted this story in my head just a few seconds earlier.

Max Barnes looked at me as if *I* had escaped from a mental institute.

"I'm sorry but I have no idea what you're talking about. I've got lots of other things to worry about right now," he said. "You should probably call the police. I doubt your brother had a ticket to the show," he said.

"He has this fantasy about being a great pilot. He was once on an airplane and persuaded the pilot to let him get at the controls. The plane nearly crashed," I said, watching his face for a reaction.

This time my words hit home. "What does your brother look like?" asked Max, his face clouded with concern.

"He's kind of short, about 5 foot 8 inches, blonde hair and brown eyes," I said, describing Nathan.

"Is his name Nathan?" asked the manager. I nodded.

"He seemed like a very knowledgeable pilot," said Max Barnes, shaking his head. "He seemed really together. He talked a blue streak about flying."

"Well, he is. I mean he was. But he had a breakdown. In either case you cannot let him fly that plane tonight!" I said, losing my cool a little. Max Barnes looked suspiciously at me.

"How did you get in here again?" he asked slowly. "This all feels a bit odd," he added.

"I got a ticket to the show. Please. Don't let him fly that plane. If he does, something terrible will happen," I said.

Max Barnes slumped down in a chair by his messy desk. On the wall behind it were pictures of many other 1950s stars that had performed at the Surf Ballroom.

"Today's been pure magic except that Holly has been totally cranky about the weather and the bus. He's been cursing about that stupid bus and its heating problems since the band rolled in earlier. And then they started insisting on chartering a flight," Max said more to himself than to me.

"I didn't know what to do at first. I don't know any pilots around here. But then that young guy just walked right in during the sound check. He started talking about aviation like there was no tomorrow. He said he'd been flying all his life, had thousands of hours under his belt, and would do the job for nothing. He just wanted the opportunity to fly the great Buddy Holly," he said shaking his head.

"I thought to myself, how lucky was that? And then I called the local airfield and rented a plane right on the spot," he said.

"You can't let him take them," I said swallowing hard. I didn't want to rock Max's world and tell him that nobody would survive the flight.

We heard the concert going strong in the ballroom. "After setting up the flight, I finally had a chance to go and enjoy the show," he said wistfully. "But then I realized I had to come back here to line up a car to get them to the airfield. And that's how I found you," he said glaring at me again.

"I know a bit about flying myself...I fly too," I said. Well, it was the truth, sort of. I was an aviator, just not the conventional kind. I was a musiator.

"Fine, then you can fly the plane!" said Max Barnes.

"No, wait!" I started to protest.

"It's either you or your brother," said Max.

"Okay," I said, not believing what I had just done.

CHAPTER NINE

Flight Song

I never did see Nathan that night. After our conversation, Max Barnes told Nathan that he wasn't going to fly Buddy Holly, and he fled the ballroom. I tried to find him but I couldn't and Max Barnes told me it was time to get over to the airfield.

I wished my life could be like other teenagers as we headed over to the airfield. I didn't know why I had agreed to fly this mission. I hoped I could morph myself out of there before I got to the airfield. I knew I couldn't change history. I'd learned that on past journeys to Musicland. One cannot change history, just live it in this alternative universe an octave away from reality. In any event, I knew that Amadeus had told me to stop Nathan from getting on that plane and that's what I'd done. Agreeing to fly myself had seemed like the easiest way to accomplish that, or so I'd thought.

What followed was an experience that would forever change my life. It would color the way I see things, the way I feel about music, about flight, about love and about life itself.

I got to the airstrip before the musicians. I was the first to arrive on the tarmac where the single-engine Beech Bonanza was parked. Something stirred in me when I looked at that plane. Despite the horrible fate I knew lay ahead for the musicians, I couldn't wait to get up in the air.

It was a strange sensation, not unlike the way I felt about music when it was taking over my entire body. It was almost like the way I'd felt in the hangar earlier, unable to control my urge to play my keyboard. Pilots and musicians were a lot alike, I realized. It was true.

I couldn't deny the thrill I felt as I looked at this airplane, admiring its sleek form, its graceful lines that exuded power. With the sudden expertise of a seasoned pilot, I examined everything from the wheels to the windshield, as if I'd had flight training for years. Everything seemed to check out.

And then I climbed into the cockpit, taking it all in with this newfound sensibility. The dashboard with its various dials and switches, the smell of gas, leather and metal were all familiar and inviting. I gripped the controls and imagined taking flight.

And then as if I was possessed by the soul of a pilot, I revved up the engine, hearing it cough to life. The propeller started to whirl and moved so fast it became a blur.

Hearing the surging engine awakened something in me. My heart ached to be airborne. Yes, this was what it was like to be a pilot, a person born dreaming of flight. It was like being moved by music that spoke directly to your soul. I wanted to savor this feeling, get drunk on it. But then I forced myself to cut the engine. I had to wait for the others.

And soon none other than Buddy Holly himself approached the plane, offering me his hand.

"I didn't realize a girl was flying tonight," he said with a smile. His handshake was firm. I couldn't believe I was shaking hands with Buddy Holly!

A few minutes later Ritchie Valens and the Big Bopper joined us, although Valens took the form of a human-like jaguar and the Big Bopper was a big chimp. They both climbed aboard, settling into their flight positions. I started to panic. I didn't want to fly them to their deaths here in Musicland. I didn't want to die either. I felt chords returning to my brain and prayed it was a song that would take me away from here. But I also had the strongest urge to fly. I felt truly divided between flight and music.

The weather was snowy and cold. The sky had poor visibility. And I felt nervous as my body willed me to start the engine again. The propeller began to whirl as did my heart in anticipation of the imminent journey which I knew would be ill-fated.

I taxied the aircraft toward the runway, feeling dread with every second. Buddy and the others were blissfully unaware of their fate, totally excited at the prospect of flying to their next gig.

A voice crackled over the radio. "Bonanza Three-Zulu-Yankee, this is Mason City Tower. You're cleared for takeoff runway one-five. After takeoff, climb to 500 feet, turn right, heading two-four-zero, climb and maintain three thousand. Departure control will be on one-two-four-point-six-five."

I spoke into the microphone as if this was the most natural thing in the world, yet still wondered how I had acquired these skills.

"Roger Bonanza Three-Zulu-Yankee cleared to go. Runway one-five, climb to 500 feet, turn to heading two-four-zero," I said indicating that all systems were go. I advanced the throttle to attain maximum takeoff power, and the plane sped down the runway, bouncing slightly.

I couldn't have stopped the plane if I tried. A need to be airborne had taken wing inside me. Again, I understood why pilots lived their lives in pursuit of this dream with every waking moment. But I just wished this revelation wasn't happening to me there and then.

I felt the plane start to lift but any feeling of joy was soon obliterated by a huge clump of snow that blinded the windshield. I felt myself lose control of the plane. One of the wings hit something. The engine strained under the weight and lack of lift due to the damaged wing. We started to roll to one side. My worst fears were confirmed. When I looked over to Buddy, I saw in an instant that he understood what was happening.

"We're going down!" someone yelled. I held my breath as more snow filled the windshield and every muscle in my body froze.

I braced myself for impact, closing my eyes as the plane careened head-on into the icy ground. I heard metal slamming into earth, but felt no pain.

And then that horrible grating sound turned into one of the chords that had been haunting me for days. It grew louder and louder and louder. And when I opened my eyes, I found myself suspended in midair, hovering over the plane's wreckage.

I felt shame, sadness and grief at the realization that I alone had narrowly escaped the disaster. I fought revulsion as I scanned the ground below for the others, but I didn't see them. And then a new song filled my head: "Crossfire," by Stevie Ray Vaughan, the great bluesman my dad loved. Vaughan had also died in a crash in the Midwest. What did all this mean? I closed my eyes and let Stevie Ray take me skyward like a hot air balloon suddenly cut loose from its mooring.

CHAPTER TEN

Surfing

"Let's go, Zoey. Someone very special wants to see you," said Amadeus. I opened my eyes and saw that I was back in Clear Lake outside the Surf Ballroom. But it seemed different. It was quiet. I wondered where Nathan had gone.

I felt drained. A great sorrow hung over me; I hated myself for piloting the plane that had brought down Buddy Holly and the others. But in another way, I felt enlightened. I had experienced the power of flight. I felt the glory of soaring through the air. I wanted to go with Amadeus. I knew where he was taking me.

It was time to visit Mrs B. She was my music mentor, my guru in Musicland. I hoped she'd shed light on what had happened, help me make sense of it. Or at least she'd help me expand musically. For that's what always happened there. I usually came back from these visits a bit wiser and a bit better on the piano.

I followed Amadeus through the ballroom and realized the mood had completely changed. The people around me were wearing 1990s garb. And when I looked to the stage I realized Don McLean was up there, singing "American Pie."

I felt like crying as I heard the melancholy song blare over the speakers. It made me think again of my harrowing near-death experience. I wished I could have somehow prevented it from happening there in Musicland. We walked through the rear exit and into a wooded area and soon found ourselves at the entrance of a cave I knew well. We were at the place where Mrs. B lived.

We walked quietly through a long dark corridor lit by candles. We turned and started walking down another long hallway that resembled a modern office building floor, except for the fact it was made out of stone and rocks.

When I'd first come there three years earlier, I had been terrified and claustrophobic. But now I felt totally at home. We stopped at a door that was indistinguishable from the other doors. I wondered who else lived in these strange cave dwellings.

Amadeus pulled out an enormous ring of keys he had somehow concealed on his tiny furry body and opened the door. My eyes started to tear up as a large woman greeted us. Her name was Crescendo Ballad, but I called her Mrs. B. She was 6 feet tall and weighed 250 lbs and every inch of this huge person exuded harmony.

But beneath that harmonious exterior was a steely determination.

Yes, Mrs. B was my teacher, my spiritual advisor and guardian angel all rolled up into one. And she also happened to make the best tea in the world. I knew I was safe once I'd gotten to that doorway, no matter whatever perils I may have faced in getting there.

"Zoey!" she exclaimed, sweeping me into her huge, fleshy arms. "You've gotten so tall," she said, standing back and appraising me from head to toe. Her smile lit up her whole chubby face. It felt so good to be with her.

I wondered if this was what it felt like to be with a grandmother. I'd never met mine. My mother's mother had died right after I was born. And my father had never been able to track his down. His mother abandoned him when he was three. But that was a whole other story, and I didn't want to think about that. Right now, I wanted to bask in Mrs. B's glorious, harmonious love. Yes, it definitely felt like I was seeing a grandma after a long separation, I thought with a silly grin on my face.

There was so much to tell her. Mrs B. always put it all together for me. She had guided me towards the truth about my father and my own musicality three years ago. It had been painful at times. I remember crying in this very room and even fearing for my life at times.

"So you've been studying ear training?" She always knew exactly where I stood musically. "And now you've also had a bit of air training."

I nodded.

"So now you see how the passion that drives pilots and musicians can be quite similar," she said.

"Yes."

"The key to ear training is in not only opening your ears, but in opening your heart," she said. "In any case, I can't wait to hear you play and see how much you've progressed," she said.

I'd always been struck by how much Mrs. B resembled my first piano teacher, Mrs. McGuillecuty. There were a lot of parallels between life in Musicland and in Los Angeles. Everything seemed the same, I thought as I looked around. Directly ahead of me was a small den with a piano and a crackling fire in the fireplace.

It was the same piano I had at home, down to the missing N in the name above the keyboard. It said ME DELSSOHN instead of Mendelssohn, just like the one in our guest room.

I followed Mrs. B into the next room, which also looked pretty much the same. Colorful rugs and tapestries adorned the walls. One side had a tapestry of gold flowers on a maroon velvet background. On the opposite wall was another tapestry featuring Ray Charles, the blind blues piano legend, playing on a baby grand.

"I don't remember this one," I said, staring at the tapestry.

"That is the changing tapestry. You're studying ear training, right?" she said.

I nodded.

"That tapestry wall mirrors what you're studying. Many blind musicians never learn to read music. Ray Charles' wonderful piano prowess all came through his ears," she said and turned to me.

"How are you doing with your ear training?" She sat down by a small round table and motioned for me to sit on the chair across from her.

I smelled steaming Red Zinger tea from a teapot between us. My heart was still beating fast from my near brush with death, but I tried to shove the image of the crash from my mind. I was too exhausted to talk about it. Mrs B already knew about it anyway. She knew about everything that went on in Musicland.

"You're not here to just learn about ear training, are you?" she said, stirring me from my thoughts. I studied the Red Zinger flakes floating in my cup and then looked at her.

"No." I said shaking my head. Three years ago I'd asked Mrs. B about my dad, another young man who had gone missing. Mrs. B had helped me find him and had given me the tools to discover my own truth. Could she help me find Nathan?

"My friend disappeared at an air show. Do you know where he is?" I asked.

Mrs. B frowned, looking very sad. "Poor Nathan has fallen prey to a very powerful and dangerous person. Some musicians break the rules in Musicland," she said.

"Why?" I felt creepy all of a sudden. Mrs. B was my rock here. It felt odd to hear her speak this way.

"These people are unhappy and greedy. They only want more power. They've been hurt badly," she continued. "When someone has this gift combined with anger and pain it can be very dangerous," she said. "And I believe that someone like that had a hand in what happened to Nathan."

I shuddered. All of my worst fears rushed through my brain. "This someone musi-morphed Nathan here, right?"

Mrs. B nodded solemnly.

"And that person tried to kill him by getting him on Buddy Holly's plane?" I said.

"And he almost killed you!" she exclaimed. "Nathan was lucky…because you were there. And whoever did this to Nathan doesn't know you also have such immense power," she said with great emphasis, staring deeply into my eyes.

My heart skipped a beat. Mrs. B always righted everything that was wrong, but this time she seemed to be singing a different tune.

"Zoey, you have great musical strength, greater than most," she said. "We need you now. We need you to triumph over this evil person. His name is Tony Zapallero."

I fell back in my chair when I heard the name. Tony Zapallero was that sleazy finance guy from Cougar who had been sitting in the bleachers at the air show.

"If he succeeds in sending even one person, such as Nathan, to his death in Musicland, it will open the floodgates. If you can make someone disappear, I mean truly disappear, then you have committed the perfect crime. No one can prove anything. And if he can do that, he'll do it again. Zapallero will send scores of people here. He'll send anyone who gets in his way," said Mrs. B.

"But where is Nathan now? How can I get him back?" I stammered. This was scary. What did she mean, I had immense musical power?

"I'm not sure where he is, but if you follow your heart and ear, you will find him much in the same way you found your father. For you, my dear, it's that simple. The more you delve into your music, the closer you'll get to solving life's mysteries," she said.

"But I'm not even that good on the piano," I mumbled.

"I've told you before. You possess extraordinary talent and musical instinct. You'll be very well-known and not because of whom your dad is," she said.

I felt myself floating off into another place. Whenever I felt alone or disconnected, I floated in this nether land. I threw myself into my music. The music always pulled me back, comforted and anchored me. The chords were ringing again in my head, but I strained to listen to Mrs. B.

"I suspect you'll write a jazz opera one day, but for now you need to practice that ear training," she said, rising from her chair and heading into the room with the piano.

"Forget about everything else but your craft," she said in her sing-song voice. "Now let's play 'American Pie' by ear, shall we? And then I want to hear 'Peggy Sue' by Buddy Holly," she said, waiting for me to sit down on the piano bench, acting like this was just a regular piano lesson.

I lowered myself, staring at the keys, trying not to think about Nathan. I told myself that if I listened to Mrs. B and focused on the music, it would all work out.

"It is ear training that will advance you to your next level musically and that will also strengthen your hand against Tony Zapallero. Think back to what you've heard today. Think back to what you were hearing when Nathan disappeared. And you'll find a clue…" she said tinkering on the keys, playing the first few riffs of the song.

"He was there at the Surf Ballroom. But I couldn't find him," I said.

She put her finger to her lips to silence me. "No more talking for now. Just play."

I played "American Pie" from start to finish, surprising myself at how well I sounded and how good it felt. I pictured Buddy Holly as I'd just seen him on stage, rocking and rolling in all his glory.

I felt like I was back in the Surf Ballroom in 1959 as I played the song. It felt so real, I forgot everything around me. I kept playing the music over and over and over again. I closed my eyes and let the music transport me.

And then when I opened my eyes, I found myself in the hangar in Oshkosh. It was 1 in the morning and everything was still.

CHAPTER ELEVEN

Getting the Hangar Out of It

I sat there staring at the spot where Nathan had stood on the day of the Silo demonstration.

John Kiefer had been so quick to make sure only Nathan would fly. I had found it curious to see him so defensive about it. I heard footsteps.

I realized how vulnerable I was out here all by myself. Who was coming? Could it be Tony Zapallero? The footsteps grew louder and I felt a wave of fear as the door opened. The cute guy who'd been sitting near Zapallero on the bleachers walked in.

"What are you doing here?" He seemed more nervous than me and genuinely shocked to find someone else there. He didn't seem threatening, although I knew I shouldn't trust anyone associated with Zapallero.

"I forgot my backpack and then I got the urge to play," I said, putting my keyboard away, trying to act like this was the most normal thing in the world. I know I must've looked pretty kooky. What kind of weird girl comes out all by herself to play keyboard in a hangar in the middle of the night? If he even knew the half of it, I thought.

"I heard you playing. You sound good," he said, grinning. He was a real hottie with blonde curly hair and green eyes. If he didn't hang out with Kiefer and Zapallero, I would have fallen for him right then and there.

"What do you make of what happened today?" I asked. If I couldn't trust him, I might as well see what information I could get out of him.

He looked at me curiously. "That's what I'm trying to find out. I know that this was not supposed to happen," he said. "My name's Joe Leonard, what's yours?" He offered his hand.

"Zoey." I shook his hand, looking away. It was hard to stare him in the eye without blushing.

"So what was supposed to happen?" I asked, getting annoyed with myself for having a crush in such a serious situation.

"He wasn't supposed to disappear mid-flight! He was just supposed to fly the Silo," he said.

"Do you play an instrument?" I asked.

"No," he said, surprised by my question. Now I was certain he thought I was loopy.

"Does anyone at Cougar?" I asked, taking in his broad shoulders. I'd never stand a chance with this guy.

"Kiefer plays the bass," he blurted, looking stricken. "What does that have to do with anything?"

He stepped back a little. Yup, he was probably thinking I was nuts. I couldn't blame him. But it didn't really matter what he thought. I needed to save Nathan.

"Does Kiefer keep a bass around here?" I persisted.

"No. Why would that matter anyway?" He was even cuter when he got annoyed. But I knew I shouldn't push it. "I'm not sure, but it might," I said.

"Well, that's pretty weird," he said combing his hair back with his hand.

"What is?"

"Well, things did change a lot at Cougar. And it all started to happen when Kiefer brought his bass into the office," he said, looking at the spot where the Silo had been.

"Did Zapallero play an instrument too?" I felt like I was really hitting on something.

"No, but he was the one who got Kiefer started. It was strange. Kiefer and Zapallero went out one night and the next day, he brought a bass into the office and started playing it a lot. Nothing like that had ever happened before. It's a pretty buttoned-up corporate environment," he said.

I waited silently for him to continue.

"What's that got to do with Nathan Gordon?" he said staring me in the eye.

I got a feeling something really strange was happening at Cougar, but I still didn't know how much I should trust

Joe Leonard even though he seemed like a good guy. "I think Zapallero has some strong...connections in the music business," I said slowly.

"You mean like he's in with gangsters?" asked Joe.

"Could be. My dad's in the music business too and he's said a few things," I said, lying. I doubt my dad had ever even heard of Tony Zapallero. But I was on a roll. "Had you ever met Nathan before?" I asked.

"No. Had you?" he asked.

I shook my head. "I only met him and Ruby yesterday," I said, sighing. "This has been the longest day."

"Yeah," Joe agreed. "Hey, I'm starving," he said suddenly. "I know where they make the best blueberry pancakes in the world. Want to go?"

I nodded amazed at my good fortune. Was this cute guy really asking me out?

"Good," he said. "And besides, we've got to get out of here before the Feds get here. If there's a mob connection, they're probably on to it already," he said.

I still had my doubts about Joe Leonard, but staring at those big green eyes over pancakes sounded perfect. And for now, he was buying the theory that Zapallero was probably involved with organized crime. Maybe I could get more information about Cougar from him over breakfast.

I doubted that Joe Leonard could even comprehend the concept of musi-morphing, but I would soon find out that there was more to Joe Leonard than I thought.

A little while later, we sat in a booth at a greasy spoon called The Great Lakes Diner, devouring the most divine blueberry pancakes I'd ever tasted.

We didn't talk much at first. The enormity of Nathan's disappearance and my harrowing flight in Iowa had caught up with me. I was so tired all of a sudden. But two cups of coffee and Joe Leonard's company re-energized me.

"Are we close to Cougar?" I asked. Mrs. B had said to follow my instincts and something told me that I may find some clues at Cougar. I knew there had to be a connection between Kiefer's bass playing and Nathan's disappearance.

"We aren't far from Cougar," said Joe, adding, "So you think Cougar's up to something?" he said.

"Yes," I said.

"Me too," Joe said.

It was getting harder for me to distrust him. He didn't seem like a bad guy. He seemed really nice, in fact. It wasn't that common to meet a guy with such great looks who seemed like a nice person too. "How long have you worked there?" I asked.

"All of my life. My dad started the company with John Kiefer. He died a few years ago. I have an open offer to run the company, but I'm in college now and not sure that's what I want to do," he said.

Wow. A college dude. I felt myself falling even harder. Help!

"Sorry about your dad," I said.

"Thanks."

"What year are you?" I asked.

"I just finished freshman year," he said. "How old are you?"

"I'm going to be 16 in a few weeks," I said blushing.

"You seem older," he said.

"I've been through a lot," I said truthfully. "What would you rather do if you don't go back to Cougar?" I asked.

"Something with computers or law," Joe answered. "I'm not even sure if the offer still stands anyway. That dude Zapallero's made no secret of the fact he'd like to buy Cougar. It had been too expensive….until now," he said sounding angry.

"What do you mean? What's changed?" I asked.

"Cougar's stock tanked today. With the Silo all but dead in the water, the company's prospects are dim. Investors think Cougar's got a lemon after banking on this new plane for years. It was already delayed. And now this happened," he said bitterly. "I don't mean to belittle your friend's disappearance. That's just awful."

I remembered Nathan and Ruby talking about the Silo and its delays. Was Nathan's demise all part of some sick stock manipulation scheme? I felt a shiver up and down my spine. Did Zapallero concoct a catastrophe to send the stock down?

No wonder they'd given Nathan the five thousand dollars in advance. They knew they'd be making that back in spades. The pancakes started to taste like sand. I swallowed more coffee to keep my food down.

"So now Zapellero's going to buy Cougar?"

"Exactly. His lawyers are drafting up the papers right now. They're going to announce it in a few days," Joe said.

"That's so evil," I muttered in disgust. "Nobody knows what's happened to Nathan, yet they're already cashing in."

Joe's face grew dark. "I had my suspicions about Zapallero but never imagined anyone would go this far. I've never met anyone so greedy. I wish I really knew what happened to your friend up there," he said.

Joe Leonard was as far away from Musicland as any Midwest college boy could be, but we had one thing in common. We both wanted to take Zapallero down. I wanted to save Musicland and Nathan, and Joe wanted to save Cougar.

I was falling hard and fast for Joe Leonard and I got the feeling that he kind of liked me too. Maybe we both realized we could help each other.

"Let's go to Cougar," he said all of a sudden, as if reading my mind. It really felt like something was happening here. We were on same wave length about Cougar at the very least.

CHAPTER TWELVE

Cougar

I checked his face just to make sure he was really serious. He was.

"Okay," I said.

"I want to show you something," he said, paying the check and getting up to leave. I followed him to his car, an old blue Honda Civic.

I couldn't believe it had only been a few hours since I'd said goodbye to Tammy. I'd been to Musicland and back barely escaping with my life. And here I was with Joe Leonard on zero sleep and heading over to the Cougar Aviation headquarters at three in the morning. Cougar was over in Monroeville, about thirty-five minutes away from the air show.

I needed to sleep at some point, but this was far too important and I figured I had a good six hours before Tammy or anyone would be looking for me. Tammy could easily sleep until noon on any given day. Dad or Mom could always call me on my cell if they needed me. They'd probably call as soon as they heard about the bizarre event at Oshkosh.

But then I thought of Ruby. She would need me when she woke up. I wanted to get back to Ruby, but then I reasoned that I'd be more help to her if I went over to Cougar to check things out. I hoped to shed some light on Nathan's disappearance. It was not really a disappearance. It was merely a departure, I assured myself.

Nathan had gone on a journey from which he would return. I had managed to return and so would he. He just needed a helping hand from someone and I guess that someone was me, I thought as we drove along a country highway in the pre-dawn hour. Wisconsin was quite beautiful this time of day.

I admired Joe's profile as he drove. "Do you like school?" I asked, attempting small talk.

"I love it," he said.

"I get the feeling you wouldn't go back to Cougar even if you could."

"My dad and John Kiefer started the company twenty-five years ago, so it's kind of a part of me. You're right. I'm not sure I want to work there, but I'd hate to see it fall into the hands of a guy like Zapallero." He said the financier's name with disgust.

"What do your parents do?" he asked, changing the subject.

I wiggled uncomfortably in my seat. "My mom's a professor and my dad's a ...music producer," I answered lightly.

"Oh yeah, you said he was in the music business," Joe said.

"Were you close with your dad?" I asked, trying to steer the discussion away from my dad. I wasn't lying but I was omitting some big truths. I felt bad that I was questioning my trust for Joe when I was the one who was being dishonest.

"He was a great guy and a good pilot. He built Cougar up from scratch," he said. "We've had ups and downs, but things have really changed with Zapallero."

Joe turned off the highway and drove through a residential area.

"It's like Kiefer fell under this guy's spell," he said.

"Well, I know a lot of people who keep instruments at their office. But you're saying that was a pretty weird thing to happen at Cougar?"

"Definitely, Kiefer was one of the most hardworking executives I've ever known. It would never occur to him in a thousand years to play his bass during working hours. That's not him," he said. "Do you think Zapallero promised him a record deal or something? He definitely got John off his game at Cougar."

"Maybe," I said, considering this theory. I didn't know how Zapallero had gotten Kiefer to change. He must've promised him something. Or maybe Kiefer was scared into cooperating.

"We're here," said Joe as we drove up to a building that bore a sign saying COUGAR. "Come on, I'll show you around. I'll take you to the Cougar Aviation music studio," he said, parking the car.

It was eerily quiet and deserted this time of the morning. I felt a chill even though it was still quite warm outside.

CHAPTER THIRTEEN

Funny Business

I would later discover that Kiefer was merely a pawn in Zapallero's scheme to manipulate people to their deaths in Musicland.

Just as we arrived at Cougar headquarters, John Kiefer sat in his living room across town. He was staring at the TV, but saw nothing on the screen. He was terrified, thinking about what happened during the Silo demonstration in Oshkosh. The phone rang and he jumped. He picked up, hesitantly.

"I'll be right down," he said, turning off the TV and heading out of his condo. Nervously he punched the button for the elevator. The elevator doors opened. Moments later, he was walking across the garage below his apartment building towards a black town car.

Kiefer told me he felt like he was walking to his own execution as he approached the car in the garage. Zapallero sat in the back seat. The rear passenger seat window rolled down.

"Come sit with me for a few minutes," snarled Zapallero from inside the car, sounding jovial and vicious at the same time. Kiefer, relieved at hearing this would only take a few minutes, opened the door and slid next to the gangster. Kiefer handed Zapellero an envelope.

"It's all here?" said Zapellero greedily tearing open the envelope. He grunted in satisfaction.

"Yes," said Kiefer, trying to sound cool. Inside he felt so nervous he was afraid his bowels might explode at any second.

"I want the rest this week," said Zapallero, sucking deeply into his cigar and then exhaling smoke into Kiefer's face. Kiefer tried to hold back a cough but it only made him choke. He started to wheeze.

"I can't do that," he said, wiping away tears from his eyes. Zapallero smirked and stared a long time at Kiefer.

"You have no choice," he said, blowing more smoke in his face and flicking ashes on Kiefer's black pants. Kiefer coughed harder this time, sending ashes all over the car.

"I just need a little bit of time. It's taking a little longer to get the papers drawn up in Washington," he said, afraid to look Zapallero in the eye.

Grunting again, Zapallero looked over disgustedly at Kiefer and then made a face that said, "It figures." John Kiefer braced for more torture.

"Wednesday then. And don't disappoint," said Zapallero, stuffing the envelope inside a briefcase. Inside were stock certificates.

"You show up with more stock certificates and a signed merger deal from your lawyer this week," he said and then nodded at a thug who leaned over from the front seat and jabbed his thumb hard into Kiefer's forehead, sending searing pain down to his toes.

Kiefer groaned and grabbed the door handle to get out of that torture chamber as quickly as possible. Luckily, nobody stopped him. Once he was standing outside the door, he turned to Zapallero, rubbing his forehead.

"Good job with the Silo! There's plenty of more work like that for you as long as you don't screw up. You're part of the team now!" said Zapallero, smirking.

"Okay, Mr. Zapallero," said Kiefer nodding nervously at his tormenter in the car.

"You can call me Zap. We're buds now. Sweet dreams Kiefer," said Zapallero, hitting the button to make the window slide up.

The driver turned on the ignition and the town car drove away fast. Kiefer heard the wheels squeal against the garage floor long after they'd gone. He later told me how he felt at that moment, how he had doubted he'd even survive the week.

He was transferring all of his stock holdings to Zapallero, which meant he was giving up the company that he and Mark Leonard had built.

He wished he'd never gotten mixed up with Zap in the first place. "I had no idea that Zapallero had these extraordinary music powers," he told me when I saw him again. Kiefer had never expected Zap's merger plan to involve murder and musi-morphing.

CHAPTER FOURTEEN

Home Bass

Kiefer went back up to his apartment and put ice on his head and thought about calling the police. But he knew it would do no good.

At that very moment, Joe and I were standing in the entrance to Cougar in Monroeville. Joe waved a security card by a panel near the door. We heard a click and then Joe opened the door. I followed him in.

There was a plane suspended from the ceiling of the lobby, like the kind you see at the National Air and Space Museum in Washington, DC.

"I helped design that plane," said Joe, proudly pointing at the aircraft. "It was the precursor to the Silo. I know every detail of those specs and there was nothing wrong with it," he said, more to himself than to me.

"Maybe someone messed with them. Maybe it was sabotage," I said, resurrecting TV cop lingo. He looked at me sideways and grimaced.

"It could be sabotage. It could've been your friend, Nathan, got some weird stroke up there that triggered some bizarre supernatural occurrence. Maybe an asteroid, that was invisible to the human eye, struck the plane."

I felt the sting of his sarcasm. He had an edge I hadn't seen before. I knew he was upset but it wasn't fair to take it out on me. I was just trying to be helpful.

"I just wondered if someone did something to the plane," I said quietly.

"You know how many things can go wrong with an airplane?" he said.

I shook my head. "I don't know half as much as you about airplanes, but I do know that people who fly love it more than life itself," I said.

"Sorry. Yeah, that's true about pilots and flying," said Joe.

"And the same could be said about people who make music," I said. "They love it more than life itself." I suddenly thought of my father with a pang. I felt bad about the way I'd left things.

"And you still think there's some music connection here? You heard that Zapallero runs in some unsavory music circles?" he asked.

"Yes," I said looking away. It wasn't entirely untrue, but it wasn't the kind of "music circles" that Joe was thinking of. "I do find it interesting that things got weird around here after Kiefer picked up the bass," I said.

I really wished I could tell him about Musicland but I couldn't. Perhaps one day Joe Leonard would find out for himself. But if I told him, I'd ruin his chances of ever going to Musicland. And even a straight-laced Midwestern college geek deserved a chance to experience it.

"Things got weird around here around the same time they decided to demo the Silo at Oshkosh," he said, walking past the reception desk to a corridor leading to different offices.

"That's when Kiefer brought the bass in?" I asked. A theory was starting to form in my mind. Had Kiefer morphed Nathan using his bass?

Joe nodded. "I didn't think the Silo would be ready for Oshkosh. So many things had gone wrong. But Zapallero brought in his guys and pushed it through," he said.

"I thought Kiefer was having some kind of mid-life crisis. I mean, Cougar was sinking fast. We were getting pummelled by Piper and Cessna. Kiefer was desperate to salvage the company. He needed a new plane to put us back on the map or we'd be finished." He opened a door to an office.

It looked like an ordinary office but when we walked in, something weird happened. I found the fluorescent light to be quite glaring.

When I turned my eyes downward away from the glare, I noticed that my fingers were a light tint of blue. It happened so fast, I assumed they were just reflecting the harsh industrial light. I looked to see if Joe was blue too but he wasn't. I looked again at my hands and now they looked normal. Maybe I was just tired, I thought.

I walked over to see a photo on the wall that Joe was studying. It showed a young boy and a man by an airplane.

When I looked closely I realized it was Joe. He was about twelve years old in the photo. Cute kid.

"That's me and my dad," he said softly. "That was at the Oshkosh air show about seven years ago." I wanted to give him a hug all of a sudden.

He turned towards me and I thought I saw a spark in his eye. Did he like me too? I'd never had a boyfriend before and was totally pathetic when it came to reading guys' cues. I was so boyfriend-delayed.

Maybe it was because there weren't any guys around when I was growing up. It had always been just Mom and me in the house. I felt a terrible sadness all of a sudden. I missed Dad. I had wanted a father all of my life and now I had one and I'd been so nasty to him. I was so messed up. And then out of nowhere, I started hearing a blues riff in my head.

I had begun morphing again. And if I'd looked at the bottom of my feet right then I would've seen they were a deep shade of blue. This time I was morphing into the blues, which would explain why I felt so melancholy. But the music vanished as fast as it had arrived.

"I'm sorry. You must really miss him," I said once I recovered my composure.

I wondered how Joe would react if he knew who my dad was. I wondered if they'd get along, I mused, trying to shove such silly thoughts aside. I had to remain focused on finding Nathan.

"Come on. I want to check out the specs," said Joe. "These days, so much more goes into the design. There's so much new technology," he said distractedly. "Any number of things can happen, even sabotage," he said, looking apologetically at me. "Sorry about before. I didn't mean to take it out on you. It's just so crazy."

"It's okay. I know this must be hard for you, especially since you put so much work into the Silo."

"I was there for the build out of the prototype. But then I had to go back to school and Zapallero came in with this big cash infusion. By the time I came back, everything had changed," he said, and then he seemed to remember something.

"What's the matter?"

"You asked if Kiefer had ever played before all this."

"Yeah, so?"

"He used to play at the Oshkosh air show. I kind of forgot that."

It did seem like Joe Leonard was beginning to see the connection between music and what had happened to Nathan at Oshkosh.

My fingers started to twitch, but I tried to ignore it. "But other than that, you don't remember him playing that much? Would you say music was important to him?" I asked, trying to get a line on Kiefer.

"We all knew he was talented. But flying and Cougar were his life," he said.

"Does he have a family?"

"No. Work was everything to him," he said. "Come on. I want to see the specs and the files." He led me out of the office.

I wanted to see the files too but I was more interested in finding musical evidence that might explain what happened.

I followed Joe down the hall and he scanned his card to open another door.

"This area is highly restricted. Only a few top execs are allowed here. It wasn't always like that. Before Zapallero came on board, we had a real community here. It was like a college campus," he said.

I followed Joe into another ordinary-looking office hallway painted antiseptic white with doors on either side.

The first door said "Control Room," while a door right past it had a sign that said "File Room." A third room said

"Practice Room," which stopped me in my tracks. This felt like a message of sorts. All my musi-morphing had started in a practice room. I'd first travelled to Musicland by way of a practice room at Harlan University. Joe walked towards the file room but I couldn't take my eyes off the practice room door.

Another blues riff blew through my head. This time I knew what was happening. I wondered if I was going to morph right then and there.

I looked through the small window on the door into the practice room and saw a bass guitar sitting upright on a stand. I had the strongest urge to pick up the bass and lay into some blues. Joe had returned from the file room and was looking at me oddly. I must have had a weird look on my face.

"You okay?" he asked slowly.

"I'm fine," I said, trying to sound matter-of-fact.

"I told you Kiefer started acting strangely. Somehow he got the guys to build this practice room down here in the most frenzied weeks before the air show," Joe said. "It seemed totally bizarre to me. I objected to it, but Zapallero and Kiefer had some kind of weird agreement going on," he said.

"And Kiefer had this obsessive need to make music, right?" I said.

Joe looked at me suspiciously. "Yes. How'd you know? I was busy with finals so I wasn't around much. But that's what the others told me."

"Well, I kind of understand that obsessive need to make music. I'm the same way." I smiled, hoping this lame explanation would satisfy him. "It's like a pilots' need to fly," I said. "You fly, right?"

"Yes. I do and I love it." He stared right into my eyes. "Maybe there is a connection between this music business and the Silo," he said, waving the card to open the control room door.

We walked into a room that was mostly empty except for a control panel by a large window overlooking a field outside. I was getting antsy. "Is it okay if I go into the practice room for a little while?" I asked.

"Sure, knock yourself out," he said. He walked me back to the corridor and waved his card to open the door to the practice room.

"I'll be back in a few minutes. I want to check out something in that control room," he said. I felt like I should be more interested in what he was investigating but the practice room was drawing me towards it like a magnet.

I walked in and immediately got a creepy feeling. The room reminded me more of a sterile hospital laboratory than a music practice room. I felt evilness in here.

I walked over to the bass and started strumming. I tried to picture what had occurred in here. How did it work? Did someone musi-morph Nathan from here? Did Zapallero control Kiefer like a puppet?

I heard footsteps approaching and Joe entered the room.

"Have you found anything? Any musical clues?" he said.

I studied him, wondering if he might know more about musi-morphing than I thought. But from the look on his face, it didn't appear as if he did.

"No. But I do think Nathan's alive and I might be able to save him....with music," I said, immediately regretting those last two words.

But I didn't have to worry because Joe didn't understand what I meant anyway. "You think we can nail him through your connections in the music business? Poor guy was definitely in the wrong place at the wrong time. Zapallero must have thrown a lot of money at someone in special effects to pull this off," he said.

"Yup," I agreed. It was an interesting theory but I don't think what happened to Nathan had to do with slick cinematography.

"How well do you know Nathan?" he asked.

I saw where he was going with this. "You think Nathan's in on it?"

"Anyone can be bought at the right price," he said.

It was another interesting theory and one I might have believed myself if I wasn't familiar with the power of musi-morphing. "There's no way that Nathan could have been involved," I said with conviction. "I think Zapallero's goals extend far beyond Cougar and I think Nathan is in great danger," I added.

I looked at the bass, wondering how a person could morph someone else into an alternative universe. I had barely managed to get myself back and forth from Musicland with some very close calls on more than one occasion. Had the Silo been hooked up to the bass in this practice room somehow? Or had something been done to Nathan here the night before his demo? I felt that something very strange had occurred in this room. But I didn't realize that it was happening to us right then, as we stood here. We didn't know it, but whatever had been done to Nathan had already started to work on us the minute we had entered that practice room.

CHAPTER FIFTEEN

Morning After

Joe showed me around the rest of Cougar but nothing seemed as intriguing as the practice room. It was getting near the time that some early shifters may be heading into work, so we decided to leave. We got to the campgrounds just as the sun was rising. Joe was very quiet. I didn't want our "date" to end. I was going to miss him the minute we said goodbye. Would I ever see him again?

The last few hours had been among the most bizarre and magical in my life. The terror I had felt in the plane with Buddy Holly still hadn't entirely left me. But in a way, it had transformed me.

I realized that part of me had been asleep, emotionally detached. After my brush with death, I felt like I had been awakened to a new clarity that was as energizing as it was terrifying. I had encountered evil of a magnitude I never had fully comprehended. But with that came a growing appreciation of life and all its beauty. My mind kept returning to my father. I missed him, although being with Joe awakened something new inside me too.

Three years had passed and now I was back to musi-morphing again and in a deadly race to save my friend. But at the same time, I was falling for Joe. Everything was so confusing. I felt overwhelmed by the rush of conflicting emotions. For the first time, I had met someone I connected with but I knew he was clearly way out of my league and was heading back to college across the country.

All this raced through my mind as we sat quietly in the car. After spending hours with Joe, I suddenly felt myself at a loss for words. He seemed lost in his own thoughts too. I glanced at myself in the mirror and my heart sank. What had I been thinking? All hope vanished. I looked terrible! My hair was stringy. My makeup had long worn off, even though there were some messy little smears, which made it even worse.

I shrank into myself, leaning towards the passenger door. I felt super awkward now. But then something glorious happened. After he stopped the car, Joe Leonard leaned over and kissed me. Right on the lips! My first real kiss. And it was amazing. Joe Leonard had to be the best kisser ever. It felt so natural kissing him back and I couldn't stop once we got started. It was a very long and sweet kiss. Finally, he gently pulled away.

"I know you know more, but I'm not sure I want to hear it because it doesn't sound like something I'd understand," he said softly.

I was speechless. Could I wrap this guy up and bring him back to LA? I didn't know what to say. He was right. I was holding back a lot of information.

"I want to help you get to the bottom of it. I know it's important for you to clear your father's company," I said, looking away but still feeling the tingle of his lips on my lips.

"Do you think your father could help?" he asked, immediately waving a red flag. My cheeks burned with embarrassment. Was that was this was all about? Was he just trying to butter me up because he thought my dad was a big shot in the music business?

But then my heart melted again as he squeezed my hand. "We should get some sleep," he said.

I felt guilty for being suspicious. I was the one who hadn't been truthful.

I opened the car door, turning to him shyly. "Bye," I said, not daring to look him in the eye. But when I finally did, he looked back at me with those warm eyes.

"I'll see you later," he said, and squeezed my hand again. I got out of the car feeling dizzy and light-headed and then watched Joe drive away. I walked through the campsites in the early morning light. I got to our tent and everything was quiet. I peeked inside the tent and Tammy and Ruby were both out cold.

There was no point in disturbing them, I thought, checking my own watch. It was 5:30. Maybe I could catch a few winks. I lie down in my sleeping bag and fell asleep in less than thirty seconds. A mere seventy-five minutes later, Tammy was shaking me frantically.

"Zoey Zoey! Wake up. They think they've found something."

CHAPTER SIXTEEN

Clue in Clear Lake

Police found what they believed was Nathan's jacket. But the weird thing was that they found it all the way over in Clear Lake, Iowa, the same Clear Lake where I had just been—sort of.

Tammy, Ruby and I were briefed by the police outside our tent. Nathan's parents were no longer alive. He had no family to speak of. I wondered if this is why Zapallero had chosen him.

Nobody could explain how Nathan's jacket had gotten all the way to Clear Lake. There was no trace of him or anything else besides his red jacket there. The search party was now packing up and heading over there.

"If you guys want to join us, we're leaving in thirty minutes," said a female police officer at the end of our briefing. I was having a hard time focusing. Was it because I was tired or because I was musi-morphing again? I heard the officer's words but her lips seemed to be going half a frame behind each word.

I felt detached as I watched her speak. I imagined her singing the blues in a sultry voice. I looked around and everyone seemed to be singing the blues instead of talking. And then something blue kept flickering in the corner of my eye. Everything around me had a blue cast for a second.

"Zoey to Earth, Zoey to Earth," hissed Tammy in my ear. "You must have had some night with that college boy," she teased. "You look out of it!"

I scowled at her. "I'm really tired," I muttered.

"Come on. We have to pack our bags," she said and gently led me towards our tent. I absently threw things into my backpack as the blues kept running through my head. I tried to think about other things, but it was no use. The blues kept playing. It was only a matter of time before I'd be morphing my way to Musicland.

Nobody had yet made the connection between Nathan Gordon's disappearance and the Buddy Holly tragedy, but to me it was clear as a bell.

Somehow, Zapallero had linked the two aviation mishaps that were decades apart. What none of us knew at that point, however, was just how musical Nathan was. He was a very good clarinet player. He had a rare gift, one that would serve him well in his current predicament.

I thought about my own musiator powers. I knew I must've gotten them from Dad. And just then, my cell phone rang. It was him.

"Daddy," I squealed, so happy to hear his voice. But Dad didn't sound that happy back. He sounded worried.

"Zoey, are you okay? Did you see that show? I am sending a car to get you today," he said.

"I can't come back today. We're heading to Iowa," I exclaimed. It was hard to hear him or myself over the blues. This was getting old.

"What? You're going to Iowa? Why?" He sounded madder than I'd ever heard him. I swallowed hard, praying the music would stop in my head so that I could have a normal conversation.

"I'm going with Tammy and her friend Ruby, who is Nathan Gordon's girlfriend. They found his jacket in Clear Lake."

"Zoey. I don't want you getting involved in all this," Dad spat into the phone. "Wait a minute. Did you say Clear Lake?"

"Yes. We're going to Clear Lake. Dad, I'm sorry but I have to go," I said, trying to end the conversation. I tried to sound strong, although inside all I wanted to do was to go back to him and his tour. I'd never broken the code of silence with Dad but I'd seen him in Musicland, three years ago. I'd seen him from afar and up close. That was before we actually met in the "real world" in Los Angeles. I knew he was a musiator, but I didn't know if he remembered it or if he did it anymore.

"Please Dad. Don't worry. I'm fine," I said. The blues had finally given me a little break.

"You don't sound fine. Have you spoken to your mom?"

"No," I said as Tammy's dad came by our tent.

"Come on girls. We're going now," he said.

"That was Tammy's dad," I said. "We'll be travelling with him so you don't have to worry. We need to be here for Ruby," I said and then blurted, "I'm sorry about that last night in Chicago!"

There was a long silence and then he said, "Zoey. I'm sorry too. We don't need to fight. We have so much still to learn about each other."

"I know," I said, fighting back tears. "Here, why don't you speak with Dan?" I put the phone under Dan's nose with a pleading look in my eyes.

Dan took it with a smile. "Hi David. Yes, I've known Zoey since she was a baby. It's okay. This is all a little crazy. I'm just going to Clear Lake and then we'll head back. Don't worry. I've got it under control," he said, sounding very on top of things.

I fought the lump that was forming in my throat. My emotions had been on such a rollercoaster in the last twenty-four hours that I hadn't had a chance to cry. But talking to my dad had made me feel all raw inside.

Tears rolled down my cheeks as I thought about Nathan and then my dad. I never wanted to lose my father again. All my life I had searched for him. Once again I wished I hadn't left him on his tour. Everything had been fine. What happened if something terrible happened to me in Musicland and I never got to see him again?

That feeling of melancholy took hold of me again and the blues came with a dizzying intensity. I was morphing into that sad, funny, optimistic, fatalistic, catchy genre that had set the stage for many more, ranging from swing to jazz to rock and roll.

Dan handed back my phone. "He's worried about you. I think he's right. We don't want to get too deep into this. People suspect foul play. We'll just go with Ruby to identify the jacket and then let the police do their work. Do you understand, all of you?"

Ruby, Tammy and I nodded.

"So we're going to drive there today and call your dad tonight. I think he's arranging for a car to pick you up in Clear Lake. Tammy and I will be heading back to Oshkosh and then flying to Los Angeles tomorrow night," he said.

It was a four hour drive to Clear Lake. It was going to be a long day.

"Okay," Tammy and I said in unison. But it didn't turn out that way at all.

CHAPTER SEVENTEEN

Iowa

Nathan's disappearance had thrown the FBI and other authorities for a loop. In a funny sort of way, this whole catastrophe drew Mom and Dad closer. They were facing their first teenage crisis together like any normal parents would. Well, as normal as we could get.

I thought about it: a pilot goes missing and is transported to some musical universal an octave away and that's what brings my crazy musical family together.

Dad called Mom after he got off the phone with Dan. Mom had just seen the news from Oshkosh and was flipping out. Dad had never seen her this way. He'd never really seen the mother-daughter thing up close. Or even the mother thing. His own mom had skipped out on him when he was three. She'd put him on a bus at Port Authority in New York and walked away.

So he wasn't that put off at hearing my mother freaking out. It was actually music to David Peer's ears. He wanted to be with this woman, the mother of his daughter, more than ever. He was sick of parasites like Daisy who were just angling for a piece of his fame.

"Why don't you come here?" he blurted. "You'll just go crazy by yourself in Los Angeles."

"Where's here?" she asked. She didn't even know where he was calling her from. "I'm in Pittsburgh," he said.

It didn't really matter where he was. It took Mom all of three seconds before she agreed to meet Dad on tour. She had seen me and Tammy on the news standing near Ruby. Dad filled her in on the rest. Then she called me. We were already in Dan's car.

"Hi Mom," I said trying to sound as casual as possible.

"What's this I hear about you guys going to Clear Lake, Iowa?" she fired off. The significance of Clear Lake was not lost on mom. Like I said, she had taught a class on the Day the Music Died. And while she definitely did not musi-morph, she did have her suspicions. It was hard to get anything past Mom.

"They found Nathan's jacket in Clear Lake. We're going to support Ruby," I said. "I'll call you when we get there," I said.

"Zoey, I think this is a really bad idea. I just want you to know that. But I know I can't stop you so please remember to call me. I'll be with your father on the tour," she said.

It was still weird hearing her refer to anyone as my father. It had been a sore subject between us for many years. She had thought he was dead, but I'd refused to believe it. It used to infuriate her. But I turned out right after all.

And now they were together again. That worked for me. Maybe they'd forget about me as soon as they saw each other, which would be a relief. I looked out at the pretty countryside.

Ruby had withdrawn into herself. Tammy was unusually quiet too. I saw a sign that said *Clear Lake: 200 miles*. Seemed like a good time to catch up on some shuteye. I snuggled in my seat and went back to sleep.

I dreamt about playing music with Dad. In the dream, Mom was smiling in the background. But then my dream turned stressful when I found myself on a pilotless plane falling towards earth. The image jolted me out of my sleep. I opened my eyes and saw that we were in Clear Lake at a big police scene.

There were cops and reporters and all sorts of people milling around. We were right at the Surf Ballroom. Police had found Nathan's jacket in the woods behind the building. I had gone through those woods on the way to Mrs. B's.

Everything looked different now. Modern flourishes made it obvious we were not in the 1950s. Another big clue was a statue of Buddy Holly in front of the building. I rubbed my eyes. Tammy and Ruby were both sitting straight up, looking wide awake and wide-eyed at the bustling activity.

A guy in a blue jacket with NTSB embroidered on the left came over to greet us. NTSB is the National Transportation Safety Board, a federal agency that investigated air crashes. We all shook NTSB Dude's hand.

"They found the jacket behind the building. I'd like to show you where they found it. Then we'll show you the jacket. We're hoping for clues that would explain how it wound up over here," said the Dude. "Did Nathan ever say anything to you about Clear Lake?" he asked Ruby.

Ruby shook her head. "No. It only came up when we talked about Buddy Holly."

The NTSB guy glared at Ruby. "Did you guys talk a lot about Holly?"

Ruby shrugged. "Nathan's a huge fan. And he's read extensively about the plane crash. So it came up once in a while," she said.

NTSB Dude looked at her suspiciously. It was beginning to feel like they were viewing Nathan more as a suspect than a victim.

"I've seen a lot of Buddy Holly pranks in my day," said NTSB Dude.

"Nathan didn't pull any pranks," protested Ruby. "A lot of folks around here are Buddy Holly fans."

NTSB Dude had already started walking towards the statue so we weren't sure if he had even heard Ruby.

"Let's go. We found the jacket out there behind the building," he said over his shoulder. We looked at each other and followed him.

"I don't think this was a prank. Something terrible has happened to my boyfriend. He wasn't part of some Buddy Holly hoax" Ruby persisted.

"I've never said that and I'm sorry if I suggested that," said NTSB Dude, leading us through the building to an exit leading to the woods behind. Another NTSB agent, a woman, came over carrying a zip locked bag holding something red in it. I knew what it was. I could tell immediately because I recognized Nathan's red jacket.

He'd had it on the last time I'd seen him. It was made of lightweight red fleece. NTSB Girl stuck the bag in our faces. Ruby let out a gasp. It was as good as new. It was untouched. There was no question. Nathan had to have musi-morphed. How else could you explain the jacket looking so unscathed when Nathan had disintegrated like an over-microwaved piece of Swiss cheese before our very eyes?

Tammy, Ruby and Dan all stared at the jacket with disbelief. I pretended to be shocked too although inside I felt that was just the latest evidence that Nathan morphed or been morphed by someone else.

"This couldn't be," gasped Dan, looking around at the woods that stretched out in all directions. "Are we allowed to explore?" he asked.

NTSB Girl, whose name was Delores, nodded. "You can go in as long as you don't touch anything. You can go in as far as the little flags," she said, pointing to flags that had been erected around the spot where the jacket had been found.

We all started walking down a little jagged trail that led to where they'd found the jacket. "No footprints. No tracks. No fingerprints. No airplane parts. No body parts. Nothing," Delores said, as if she'd clicked off this list before.

Ruby winced on the words "body parts." And then something flashed right by my feet, which made me stop. The others had gone ahead and were walking around the little flagged area. I looked down to see where the flash had come from. And it happened again. Suddenly Ruby was by my side. She had noticed the white flash too. But when we looked down, all we saw was a white rectangular card.

Ruby picked it up. It was a concert ticket. Ruby gasped and showed it to me. It was a very old concert ticket that looked brand new. It said WINTER DANCE PARTY, Feb 2, 1959.

"He was here," Ruby said, looking into my eyes. And then, all of a sudden, I knew that she knew. And it would be okay to break the code of silence. All you needed was one clue and that ticket was our clue.

CHAPTER EIGHTEEN

Winning Ticket

If you were with someone and you both saw and understood a clue, a token or some sort of link to Musicland, then it was okay to break the code of silence. In that instant, when we both looked at the ticket, we both knew. I knew without a doubt that Ruby recognized the ticket for what it was. She knew it was from Musicland. And I knew she was a musiator.

Tammy had been right. She had said Ruby and I shared something. She said Ruby had reminded her of me, particularly when it came to her love of flying. Tammy said it was like my passion for music. She was right about that too. Flying and music are what Ruby and I had in common. But not in the way that Tammy suspected.

Tammy herself had actually morphed twice, but she was the kind of musiator who forgot her journey as soon as she crossed back over. They called her a "grace note" in Musicland. So I never talked about it with her. I didn't want to stop her from doing it again. I knew I'd find myself there again with her someday.

But it didn't look like she was clued into what was happening with Nathan. In fact, she seemed rather oblivious as she darted between the flags and rocks a few feet away with a puzzled look on her face.

I thought about all the work that Ruby and I had to do. Knowing I had a partner made me feel so much better, so much more empowered. Finding Nathan was only the tip of the iceberg. Mrs. B had said I had to save Musicland. That was crazy but nothing about Musicland was ever normal.

At least I had an ally. I thought of my dad again. I wished he were here. He might also be a grace note like Tammy, possessing no memory of his experiences in Musicland. But I wasn't sure. I just know that we'd never talked about it. Something gave me the feeling, though, that he could help if he were here. It would be a mistake, though, to put my father into danger, I thought as I got that strange sensation again.

The blues were back. It was strange but calming at the same time. I found the simplicity of the blues to be very relaxing. Almost all blues had the same structure, consisting of a line, statement or a question. The line or hook was repeated over and over with a slightly altered harmony. And then a rhymed answer arrived, giving it a satisfying resolution.

I was hearing "Crossfire," Stevie Ray's epic blues single. One of Stevie Ray's riffs washed over me, conjuring up an image of the Texas blues man in a helicopter. I shivered. He had died in a helicopter crash.

"Look!" whispered Ruby, pointing at my arm. I peered down and gasped. My entire arm was blue. I willed myself to shove the blues and air crashes out of my mind and the feeling subsided. My arm turned back to normal.

Some FAA people came over to talk to Ruby. Both the FAA and the NTSB were coming up empty-handed in the case of Nathan Gordon. Ruby seemed calmer now as they questioned her. I hoped we'd be able to be alone soon so that we could discuss some sort of plan. The Feds finally walked away, but then Tammy and Dan walked up to us.

"We need to eat. I'm starving," said Dan. I felt the concert ticket in my jeans to make sure I hadn't imagined it. It was there all right.

Once back in the car, I tried to get more information from Ruby. "What else did Nathan like? Musically, I mean?" I asked. She and I were sitting in the back. Tammy was with her dad in the front seat.

"He liked a lot of things," said Ruby in response. "But I never knew he played anything. I didn't know that he was musical until yesterday when you asked me if I played an instrument and he said he played the clarinet in high school," she said.

The police told us that Nathan had gone over to Cougar the night before his Silo flight to jam with John

Kiefer. Nathan had played clarinet until the wee hours of the morning, which had been a shock to Ruby.

We started texting each other so the others couldn't hear us. Through these texts I got a sense of Ruby's story. Like me, she thought her musi-morphing days were over now that she had found what she had long been searching for. She had found love and happiness with Nathan. And she had found another true passion in flying.

Ruby had never suspected that music and aviation would collide so catastrophically in her world. She'd been to Musicland once a few years earlier at a sad time in her life.

But once she met Nathan, the whole experience had started to feel like a distant dream -- until now.

The night before Nathan's Silo demo, Ruby had gone to sleep in the tent, expecting him by 11 pm. She had felt a premonition of sorts related to Kiefer. Something had made her nervous from the start, but she couldn't put her finger on it until she saw Nathan disappear right before her eyes.

Finding the ticket and connecting with me in this way had given her hope. And it had given me hope too.

A plan was starting to form in my brain as the blues started up again. We both put our phones away. We had been texting for a while.

Hearing the blues wasn't an altogether unpleasant feeling, but it was distracting. I tried to ignore them as I searched my backpack for a worn textbook that my friend Anna had given me. I silently cursed myself for not suspecting this earlier. I should've figured something was up when Anna handed me the book.

I made a mental note to ask her about that the next time I saw her.

"This book is a good guide for travels," she had said. I thought she was referring to my father's concert tour. But nothing with Anna was ever a coincidence. Anna was the musiator who had led me to Musicland. And now I realized that she must've known I'd be musi-morphing again this summer and would need the book for this journey. Why hadn't I read the clues? Had she known that trouble was brewing in Musicland?

Anna had been in the practice room at Harlan three years ago. She left me alone in the room when I morphed for the very first time. And Anna was the one who told me about the code of silence.

How could I have thought Anna was just encouraging me to study? Everything that had happened during the past few weeks now seemed like it had all happened for one reason. Nathan. He was the reason, I realized as I thumbed through the textbook. I looked up the blues. There were many references. I turned to the first page with text about it.

"What are you looking up?" asked Tammy looking back over her shoulder.

"The blues," I said, wiggling my toes. My feet felt a little funny. I peeked at the space between my jeans and my running shoes and sure enough, my ankle was blue. Ruby saw it too and rolled her eyes. Luckily, Tammy couldn't see it from where she sat.

I started reading about the origin of the blues. Nobody really knew their exact origin, although some theorized the genre had begun with slaves in the American South.

Ruby was reading along with me and caught me looking at her.

"We should try to play together sometime," she said.

"Okay," I said nodding. I knew she meant we should morph together. "Let's do that," I said. We drove in silence for a while. Dan finally turned on the radio as he searched for a restaurant.

Tammy was texting and Ruby stared out the window. I could barely hear the radio over the blues. I had this irresistible urge to play. I was finding it more and more difficult to stop myself. Finally, I pulled out my keyboard and plugged in my headphones. Ruby couldn't hear what I was playing but she was watching my hands and smiling.

And that's when it happened. I morphed back to Stevie Ray Vaughan's last concert. It was August 1990 in Troy, Wisconsin. He was only thirty-five when he and his band

Double Trouble played that night for an audience of 25,000 people. Blues legends Eric Clapton, Buddy Guy, Robert Cray and Stevie's brother Jimmie Vaughan, also played. Just after midnight, Stevie Ray hopped on a helicopter that never made its destination. It was bound for Chicago but sadly crashed into a mountain minutes after take-off. The world lost a musician of epic proportions. Vaughan was at the forefront of a blues resurgence that took place in the 1980s. He paved the way with his loud swing-driven fusion of blues and rock.

His legend had only grown since his death. I knew immediately where I was when I heard that voice and his unique hard driving guitar style, which often drew comparisons to Jimi Hendrix. Now I understood why I had been "living" the blues. I had morphed back to one of the best blues shows of all time, one that would go down in infamy as Stevie Ray Vaughan's last.

I landed backstage and was immediately reminded of my dad. Stevie Ray was one of his all-time heroes.

Vaughan never learned to read sheet music. He picked up the guitar when he was ten and was playing in clubs by the time he hit high school. He finally dropped out of school to focus on music but his life was riddled by battles with drug and alcohol until he became sober in 1986. In 1989, his new *In Step* album climbed the charts, led by the number one hit single "Crossfire." By the following summer he was gone.

I closed my eyes and let the music envelop me. The band was playing "Tight Rope" another hit off of *In Step*. It was great to have the music in my head move in sync with the music outside. But then my world turned completely upside down and the next thing I remember, I was feeling panicked at the controls of Stevie Ray's helicopter.

I didn't want to fly it, but the urge to be airborne took over my body and commanded me to take the controls in my hands. It was like the sensation I had felt earlier that had compelled me to play the blues. Yet at the same time, my heart was breaking as I glimpsed back and recognized the face that I'd seen in photos so many times before.

I hated being here, but tried to overcome my emotions and focus on Nathan. I sensed he may have been at the show. Something was pulling me towards these shows, these times in history. I felt like I was one step behind him. But whoever was doing this may have the last laugh on me, I thought. Would I escape this crash? Maybe I could change history this once, I thought, as I seemed to pilot the helicopter effortlessly.

Visions of my father and my mother leaped before my eyes seconds before I found myself desperately trying to see through fog as thick as soup.

And then it was over. Just like that, I was back in Dan's rental car. Nobody had noticed a thing, not even Ruby. Time had stood still between two notes of a blues riff. And when I came back I just picked it up again. But on the inside, I felt totally wiped out. I hated myself for not stopping the helicopter. I pulled my headphones off and started weeping quietly. Ruby offered me a tissue.

This was too much. I wished I was back on Dad's tour. I looked out the window trying to stop myself from crying when a Glenn Miller tune popped up on the radio.

The music lifted my spirits. After it ended the DJ said, "And that was Moonlight Serenade by the great Glenn Miller, who was born right here in Iowa. Glenn Miller was one of the greatest Big Band leaders of his time and his death mid-flight during World War II is one of the world's biggest unsolved mysteries," continued the DJ.

The words stunned me, but nobody else was making the connection. It was plain as day to me. Wherever we turned, we were encountering legendary musicians who had died in flight.

Dan got a call on his phone. "You've got to be kidding," he exclaimed.

I looked at Ruby.

"Well, I was planning on going back to Oshkosh after lunch, but I guess we can go there," he said. This got all of our interest. As soon as he hung up, Dan told us there had been a change of plans.

"We're going to a town called Clarinda. Police there said they've found a wallet and they believe its Nathan's," he said. "They found it at the Glenn Miller Birthplace Museum," he said.

"That's strange," blurted Ruby. "We just heard him on the radio!" I nodded and eyed her to see if she was also seeing the pattern in all of this.

"Very strange. What do Glenn Miller and Buddy Holly have in common?" I asked to everyone and no one.

"They both died in plane crashes," said Ruby.

"Bingo," I said.

"Maybe this is some sick kind of hoax after all," said Tammy.

"Maybe," I said, opening my textbook to see what it had to say about Glenn Miller. There was a lot about the Big Band leader who had been a huge force in swing, an outgrowth of the blues. And then swing in turn influenced many modern day blues musicians such as none other than Stevie Ray Vaughan. The book referred to both of these musicians together several times. It said that Stevie Ray's relatives had played in Glenn Miller's band. These stories kept overlapping.

All these musicians had much in common besides the fact they had died in flight. And all of them were having a profound musical influence on me on this journey.

Mrs. B was right. If I focused on the music everything would work out. It always did. Glenn Miller's classic sound came on. It gripped me and I once again felt a powerful desire to play.

CHAPTER NINETEEN

Business Matters

As we headed towards lunch and Clarinda, Iowa, some pretty bizarre things were going down at Cougar Aviation in Wisconsin. John Kiefer had dragged himself into work on Monday wondering how he'd ever get through the day.

He went into the practice room where Joe and I had been the night before. Everything had seemed normal, he told me. Joe and I had been careful not to leave any traces that we'd been snooping around. Then late in the day, Tony Zapallero walked in.

"He should have come back by now," Kiefer said sadly. "I don't know how this happened."

Zapellero tapped his foot impatiently. "He's not coming back. He disappeared at 10 in the morning. It's been over twenty-four hours," said the tycoon.

The words hit Kiefer hard. "I would never have done this if I thought it would end this way." he said, feeling a little bolder without Zap's thugs around. Or maybe he didn't care what happened to him anymore now that his life was ruined.

"It's unfortunate, but things like this happen. Planes go down. People go missing," said Zapallero.

Kiefer looked at Zapallero to see if he was laughing. They both knew this was no ordinary situation. Thousands of people had seen Nathan go poof in a purple cloud of smoke. Millions more had watched it replayed on TV.

Even though suspicions were beginning to swirl around Cougar, Zapallero knew he had committed the perfect crime. People could suspect all they want, but all anybody could figure was that the plane that Cougar had invested millions on had turned into a giant malfunctioning piece of junk.

Kiefer told me that Zapallero had originally planned to showcase the Silo as part of his new "time travelling" technology. And bringing back Nathan would have been the big encore. But something went wrong. It didn't really matter, according to Zapallero, who had even bigger plans.

"We just need to keep moving forward. Nobody will be any worse for it," he said to Kiefer in the practice room.

"That's not what we agreed on," insisted Kiefer, surprising himself with his forceful tone. "He was supposed to be found alive. I know we can get him back. We have to keep trying."

"That used to be the plan," said Zapallero, his laughter sinister. His cackling laughter made Kiefer's head hurt. Nathan was just a small piece of Zapallero's puzzle. His experiment had worked and his technology had made it possible for him to morph people musically to wherever he wanted. That's what mattered.

"We've got to get him back," maintained Kiefer.

This made Zapallero laugh even harder, but he was getting annoyed with Kiefer. He suddenly took the bass guitar and smashed it violently on the floor, splintering it into thousands of tiny pieces.

Kiefer balled his fists but felt helpless to do anything else. Zapallero finally stopped laughing and wiped tears from his face, smiling.

"I'm joking of course. Nathan can come back. You've just got to figure out a new way to do that. And keep it to yourself," he said, starting to laugh all over again. He started to leave. "Guess it's time to pick up another instrument, Kiefer. And I want the rest of those stock certificates!" he said, slamming the door behind him.

Kiefer stood alone in the practice room. His eyes filled with tears. He had never intended for this to go this far. Zapallero had figured out a way to control people with music and nothing would stop him now.

And then Kiefer's phone rang. He would tell me later that it was the strangest call of his life. His ringtone played "Moonlight Serenade" by the Glen Miller Band. He had always been a huge fan of the Big Band era and Miller, but he was astonished when he heard the song. He had never put it on his phone. Still baffled, he answered the call.

"Kiefer. It's me. It's Nathan," said the voice on the other end.

Kiefer recognized the young pilot's voice but still suspected it was a hoax. "Who is this?" he exclaimed.

"Nathan! I swear it's me. I'm in Europe. I want to come home."

"Europe?" said Kiefer, wanting to believe it was true with all his heart. If it was true and Nathan was still alive, he wouldn't have to face murder charges after all. "Where are you in Europe? Are you safe? Are you okay?"

"I'm okay. But it's freezing here," Nathan said.

Kiefer was puzzled. It was July.

"If it weren't for the damn weather, I'd already be in Paris. I'm supposed to fly Glenn Miller over there so he can set up stuff for the rest of his band," the young man who claimed to be Nathan said.

This is when Kiefer realized that something very strange was going on. "What date is it?" he asked into the phone.

"You don't know that day it is? It's December 14, 1944 and it's cold and storming like hell. You guys really got me into quite a fix over here," said Nathan. At this point, Kiefer told me he heard some music in the background. It was "Moonlight Serenade" again.

And then he started to remember what had happened to Glenn Miller and his pilot and he got a horrible feeling in the pit of his stomach. Glenn Miller never made it to Paris. His plane disappeared on December 15, 1944 and the world lost one of the greatest bandleaders of all time. Miller was still listed as missing in action. His death had saddened and fascinated fans and aviation historians for decades. Even now, more than half a century later, his final flight was the subject of much speculation, conspiracy theories and controversy.

Kiefer realized what Zapallero was doing, much in the same way that I had figured it out. He saw that Zapallero was sending Nathan to moments in history when great musicians had died in flight.

"Just stay put. I'll come and get you," barked Kiefer into the phone. "And whatever you do, don't get on that plane!" he said. But then the phone went dead.

Kiefer stared at his cell phone, wondering how in the world he was going to get himself to Bedford, England in 1944.

He couldn't waste time. Zapallero had figured out how to send Nathan to these historic moments, knowing that Nathan would always jump at an opportunity to fly, not realizing that these flights would end tragically.

Zapallero had been obsessed with musicians who died in flight as well as oppressive regimes that banned musical expression. They had talked for hours about this. Kiefer admitted to me that he had initially enjoyed these lively discussions. He'd even done some research for the business mogul.

He hadn't realized why Zapallero had needed this information. He had thought of Zapallero as a friend, someone who had reignited his long dormant love of music.

But now he regretted the day he had ever let Zapallero walk into Cougar.

CHAPTER TWENTY

Boy in the Big Band

To witness Glenn Miller's magic live and up close was something one would never forget. Nathan couldn't believe his good luck. He had found himself in Bedford, England with Glenn Miller's army swing band during World War II.

He'd barely heard of the bandleader but savored every note of the music he had found himself immersed in. His clarinet playing just kept getting better and better. He didn't know if he was dreaming all this or if he was dead or in some twilight corridor between life and death. Had he crashed in Oshkosh? Was he in a coma?

It all seemed so real but totally unreal at the same time, he thought as he watched a wolf sitting upright a few seats away from him and playing a violin effortlessly. Nothing made any sense, but it didn't matter as he soaked in the band, the musicians and the incredible sound.

When someone had shouted out for a pilot to fly Glenn Miller across the English Channel, it had been a no-brainer for Nathan. He raised his hand immediately. And just like that, he was designated to fly the broad-shouldered bespectacled bandleader to Paris. Nathan knew that once he got his hands on a plane, he'd get himself home. He'd get back to Ruby and never leave her again.

Miller was set to take off on December 13, but the weather made that impossible. It was foggy, rainy and bitterly cold. So the flight had been delayed, the plane grounded.

Glenn Miller was planning to have his band perform live in Paris over Christmas. He was going ahead of the band to set things up. And before the band could go, it had to deliver eighty-eight recorded programs to the BBC for Miller's weekly radio show, which meant the band was right in the middle of a marathon recording session when Nathan entered the scene.

While Nathan desired nothing more than to get back to Wisconsin and Ruby, he somehow felt like he belonged here in this magical musical land. It had reawakened every music nerve and sensation in his body. He had never felt more alive than right now when he was playing in one of these amazing sessions with the Glenn Miller band.

He was experiencing a different kind of flying. He'd always loved music but his passion for aviation had so consumed him that he had put it aside. He promised himself that he'd never abandon his music again.

As luck would have it, the clarinet was the focal point of the unique Glenn Miller sound.

Miller had started out in the Twenties playing trombone. By the Thirties he'd created his signature sound by turning the clarinet, played over four Saxes, into the lead component in the band. It took the world by storm.

But then at the peak of his career, Miller decided to join the war effort. He had a vision that he would go to Europe to start up a band to boost the morale of soldiers.

Performing in Paris was to be a highlight, but Miller's flight kept getting delayed due to bad weather. And then it cleared up but his pilot caught the flu. And that's when this new clarinet player Nathan arrived and offered to fly Miller himself. The bandleader was finally set to go.

CHAPTER TWENTY-ONE

Moonlight Madness

Nathan didn't know much about Glenn Miller when he found himself in Bedford, England. But now that Kiefer had told him not to get on the plane it all made sense.

Flying Miller wouldn't get him home. It was guaranteed death. And the same went for Buddy Holly and Stevie Ray. He had been at Vaughan's last show too.

What a musical ride this had been. Nathan again wondered if he was in some musical nether land between earth and heaven. He kept brushing up against incredible musicians in this strange world. All of them had lost their lives in flight.

But Nathan wondered why everything had to happen in the same way here. He had heard someone call it Musicland. Maybe he could change history here in Musicland. Maybe Glenn Miller's fate would be different if Nathan flew him.

He didn't worry too much about himself. He thought he must be crash proof or something. He hadn't died in Oshkosh. He never even got near Buddy's or Stevie's aircraft. He had a feeling he'd make it through this in one way or another too. But there was no way anyone was keeping him from a plane if he could get his hands on one.

Nathan thought about Ruby as the guys and human-like animals tuned up their instruments. He still couldn't believe how much he and Ruby had hidden their musical pasts from one another. Again he told himself that if any good was to come of this crazy experience, it was a reinforcement of his love of music. And he swore silently to himself that if he ever saw Ruby again, he'd write a song about her.

Nathan had encountered much musical greatness in the last two days. It felt like he had left Oshkosh weeks earlier. He had come back to the Surf Ballroom after Buddy and the others had already gone to the airfield.

The manager had brusquely told him his deal was off. He called Nathan a fraud, saying he had shown no proof he was a real pilot. "I could get you arrested, but I don't feel like wasting my time. You owe me though," he said, jabbing him in the shoulder roughly with his index finger. "We need help cleaning this dump up," he said and then put Nathan to work cleaning the toilets.

Even though the bathrooms were gross, Nathan had nowhere else to go so he did as he was told. He worked late into the night, thinking of his next move as he scrubbed. He knew he couldn't last long outside. It was freezing cold in

Iowa in February. He decided to hide in the bathroom as everyone left.

When he came out a few hours later, the ballroom was pitch black and quiet. He looked for a phone. Could he reach Ruby from here?

But then the strangest thing of all happened. When Nathan passed the piano on the stage it felt like it was beckoning him to play. He had so much to do, but he couldn't help himself. He had to sit down and touch the keys.

He kept hearing the song "Crossfire" by Stevie Ray Vaughan over and over and over again. Why? It had been years since he'd played piano, but it felt like it was just yesterday as he hit the keys. The blues swept through him. He looked around nervously, but no one was around.

Stevie Ray's music filled the room and then suddenly Nathan visualized himself at the controls of the Silo. The room started to shake violently. Nathan wasn't sure if he should run or hide under the piano, but he had time for neither as suddenly there was a blinding light that blocked everything from sight.

He squinted to see through the dense fog that now filled the room and saw a face. It was Tony Zapallero.

Nathan had only met him once but the guy had given him the creeps. It had been at Cougar the night before the Silo demo. It had been a strange encounter. Zapallero had hugged him and held Nathan's face in his hands in the practice room.

"Thank you for flying the Silo," he said. Nathan had felt like he was a Mafia don or something.

Zap's face loomed over him now, expanding into the size of an enormous movie screen. Then suddenly Nathan was sinking. He didn't know where he was falling because everything was pitch dark.

Flickering lights surrounded him and then he noticed the lights moving in patterns that resembled a musical staff and notes. He was now floating between these pieces of sheet music. The notes grew brighter and brighter, finally blending into one another. He felt himself being pulled towards a pause sign that was glowing and pulsating, stretching this way or that to change its shape quickly. It grew larger as he neared it. He tried to resist its pull but he couldn't and he felt himself drawn closer and closer to the pause sign that was now yawning like a deep black hole.

He heard a loud, piercing shriek just as he was sucked into it, followed by utter darkness and silence. The silence frightened him more than the shrieking. He kept moving through the darkness and silence and then he saw a glowing purple light.

"Crossfire" played again in his head and the image of a helicopter slamming into a mountain flashed before his eyes. He knew it was Stevie Ray Vaughan's copter and he felt a terrible sadness. And then he landed on his feet with unbearable pain shooting up his legs.

He looked around and was surrounded by human musicians and those humanlike animal musicians he'd seen before at the Surf Ballroom. He was in the wind section of the Glenn Miller orchestra in Musicland.

CHAPTER TWENTY-TWO

From Holly to Miller

K iefer told me he had stared dumbly at his phone in the practice room after the call with Nathan had ended.

"How could I get there?" he had wondered aloud. Kiefer knew all about Glenn Miller. Not just about his disappearance, but about his music too.

He knew that nobody from the plane had ever been found. He had just researched the aviation mystery for Zapallero. He had thought they were bonding over dinner, but now he knew that Zapallero had just been extracting information from him and brainwashing him into being a pawn of his own twisted musical flight scheme.

Kiefer told me he had never heard of Musicland before he met Zapallero. The scoundrel had taken him to a restaurant and had put him into a trance. A few days later, they set up the practice room. Later, Kiefer would explain to me how Zapallero had used digital imagery and encoded a device with someone's musical DNA. Using this technology, he could pinpoint people with precision to certain moments in history in Musicland.

Kiefer had seen him do it. The mad scientist had done it to Kiefer, sending him back and forth to Simon & Garfunkel's 1981 reunion concert in Central Park. The folk duo's show was one of the largest concerts in history, drawing about half a million fans to the giant lawn. Kiefer had come back from the experience energized, transformed, believing Zapallero was a genius.

But then everything changed at the air show when Zapallero showed his true colors. Kiefer realized then that he had never cared if Nathan ever came back. Kiefer had seen Zapallero's madness, his greed, his power. At what point would he stop? When would someone like that be satisfied? Kiefer hated himself for assisting in such evil.

Kiefer had heard on the news that the police had found Nathan's wallet at the birthplace of Glenn Miller and that the search party was heading there.

But he feared that Zapallero was already one step ahead and already plotting his next move. Who knew where he'd send Nathan next if he didn't succeed in getting him on Glen Miller's plane?

Kiefer had even studied Clarinda, Iowa for Zapallero. He knew the town was very proud of their most famous native. There was a Glenn Miller museum there. Each summer the town held a Glenn Miller festival.

A whole industry existed around Glenn Miller even though he had moved from Clarinda when he was a tyke.

Kiefer told me he had shared all of these details with Zapallero, who had been keenly interested in Miller during their dinner.

If he'd only known what the miserable guy had been planning he would never have told him. But Zapallero would've found out some other way, he was sure.

Kiefer started humming "Moonlight Serenade" and tapping his fingers to the music. If only he had an instrument right now, he had thought, staring at the debris that had been his bass.

And then he smiled, remembering something. He glanced at his bass case.

Kiefer remembered that he had packed a harmonica there long ago. He was elated when he found it there. He pulled out the shiny little instrument from the case with great care. All the while, the music of Glenn Miller coursed through his body.

He had to get to Musicland. He had to stop Nathan from getting on that plane. He put the harmonica to his mouth and played "Moonlight Serenade," producing the song perfectly. He took one hand off the harmonica and pulled out an iPod he had secured from Zapallero's stash.

He trained his eyes on his laptop and pulled up a picture of Glenn Miller's band and pushed a button on the iPod. He kept playing all the while, focusing his mind on

Glenn Miller in Bedford, England during World War II, but nothing seemed to happen.

Had he been mistaken? Would this not work? Frustrated, he stopped playing. He didn't know what else to do but realized something strange was happening. The song kept playing in his head. He couldn't shake it.

He began playing it again, this time a little more slowly. Finally the room began to shake. Kiefer was overjoyed. Within minutes, the whole room was airborne. Kiefer knew exactly where he was headed as the room hurtled through mystical skies.

He passed through lavender-colored canyons and a night sky filled with musical instruments. After soaring through the heavens this way through several Glenn Miller songs, the practice room landed with a soft thud.

Kiefer told me he had felt like he had returned home after a long absence. I understood the sensation. He walked to the door of the room and peeked outside the window. He saw that the room was perched in a tree over a little meadow.

He remembered the first time Zapallero had sent him that he had felt like he'd gone through the looking glass. The colors were as intense and surreal as they were that first time.

But he had no time to marvel at the beauty now. He had to stop Nathan from losing his life. He had to stop him from stepping on Glenn Miller's plane.

He left the practice room and started walking through the woods and soon heard Glenn Miller's music in the air.

CHAPTER TWENTY-THREE

Iowa Sights

We were getting closer to Clarinda. And so was the rest of the world, now that word had spread about Nathan's wallet. His disappearance at Oshkosh, after all, had been dominating the news for two days now.

Conspiracy theories were flying. Bloggers speculated it was just a publicity stunt by the organizers of the Fly-In, while UFO fanatics were convinced Nathan had been stolen by aliens. The press coverage sent Cougar's stock plummeting, which is exactly what Zapallero had hoped for.

In addition to Kiefer's holdings, he had scooped up Cougar stock on the open market at bargain basement prices by the boatload.

Zapallero had no real interest in making the Silo or any airplanes for that matter. He just wanted to buy a fleet of planes cheaply to transport merchandise for his other "enterprises."

I had no real sense of what I was up against at the time. Perhaps I was distracted by Joe Leonard. It was more fun to think about that kiss. But Nathan's predicament kept bringing me back to reality.

"Tell us about Glenn Miller," said Tammy, waving her hand in front of my face. She did that when I spaced out sometimes. She'd been trying to get my attention for a while, but I guess I'd been in la-la land, thinking about Joe.

"Sorry," I managed. I had the textbook out on my lap again and I flipped to the page about Glenn Miller. My mom had a few of his albums but I hadn't listened to him that much.

"He was known for his unique clarinet-driven sound and was HUGE in his day before he went missing in a plane crossing the English Channel," I read from the book. Tammy and Ruby both shuddered.

"So many plane crashes," stated Tammy glumly. The common thread was obvious to all of us now. It was probably just a matter of time before everyone else started figuring it out.

I flipped through more pages and found a chapter about Jazz and World War II, explaining how Miller and other musicians like Artie Shaw joined the armed services to bring jazz to the troops. At the same time, Nazi Germany under Adolph Hitler, which was America's enemy, had set out to eliminate jazz. The Nazis wanted to destroy anything they considered foreign, which included Jews, Gypsies and any other people not deemed purely German as part of what they called their "final solution."

As they moved to kill millions of innocent people, they also forbade many cultural reminders of their enemies. The Nazis hated jazz in particular because it was a distinctly American genre.

I read on, fascinated to see that the Nazis in fact failed in this effort. Jazz actually flourished and spread among their youth and turned out to be a symbol of resistance.

Young jazz fans called themselves "Swing Kids" and defied the Gestapo by smuggling in records, holding secret meetings and dances and listening to the enemy's radio stations. These kids even refused to go to bomb shelters during air raids and stayed back home instead to listen to jazz. This infuriated the Nazis, and the Gestapo ultimately wound up arresting many Swing Kids.

In the textbook was a photo of a group of young men and women sitting around a table, sporting American-looking zoot suits, hairstyles and other fashion accessories that were popular in the U.S. in the 1940s. Behind them on a wall was a swastika, the Nazi movement symbol. Under the photo was the caption: Swing Kids

I read how the Nazis rounded up several hundred Swing Kids and sent some of them to concentration camps.But the Nazis didn't want the world to know about their harsh methods and so they made propaganda films in which they pretended to like jazz.

I read with horror as the book described how the Germans made one such film at a concentration camp. In the film, they showed Jewish inmates playing in a swing band. Once the filming was over, all the musicians were sentenced to death. The book showed a picture of the band with musicians wearing the Star of David pinned on their jackets. Under it a caption read: Ghetto Swingers. This was the name the Nazis had given the band.

I closed my eyes, feeling sad for all of those unfortunate musicians in the picture who were executed for no reason. And then I got a terrible feeling about Nathan. If he was anywhere near Glenn Miller as I suspected, that would place him in the middle of Europe in World War II. That could be very dangerous.

I wondered if Zapallero had a book like this too. I felt an odd beating throughout my body all of a sudden. Was I beginning to experience another musical transformation?

I looked around me. I had been reading for a while and Tammy and Ruby had both gone back to sleep. Dan was lost in his own thoughts as he drove. I looked back down at my textbook and was surprised to see it was now open to a new page.

I was now looking at a chapter about tempo, which was defined as the speed at which music is played. I had once morphed rhythmically and had walked around for days hearing a beeping sound. Nobody else heard the beeps, drums and cymbals that accompanied me. It was maddening, but I learned a lot. I learned how to figure out how many beats go into a measure in a song. Tempo determines how fast those beats are played.

In some music, the tempo remains the same throughout the song, while in others the music speeds up and slows down for dramatic effect.

As I read this, I felt the beating in my body speed up and slow down. I felt strange and exhausted. I had never morphed so much in so short a time, but I knew it was necessary if I wanted to get back to Musicland and find Nathan.

CHAPTER TWENTY-FOUR

House of Miller

The beat put me in a trance and made me fall into a deep sleep. When I awoke we were about twenty minutes away from Clarinda. The beat continued to drum in my head.

Ruby stirred. "I've been there before," she said quietly.

"What are you talking about?" I asked, startled.

"Clarinda," she replied.

I wondered why anyone would travel to Clarinda, Iowa, unless they were a Glenn Miller fanatic.

"I went to the Glenn Miller festival," she said.

"What's it like?" I was truly curious.

"It's fun. Back in the 1970s, Clarinda honored Glenn Miller by naming a scholarship after him. Anyone who studies music around here knows about it. The town holds a festival each summer for students to compete. I participated when I was in high school."

"Did you win?" Why hadn't she mentioned this earlier?

"Second place, which was two thousand dollars," she said proudly.

"Wow!" This was crazy. Nathan's wallet was found here and now it turned out that Ruby had performed there. "Will you show me where you played?" Could we morph from here? Ruby nodded with a look that said she was thinking the same thing.

"We played behind the house where he was born. Now there's a museum next to it," she said. "The festival was fun. There are bands from around the world," she said.

"I don't know Glenn Miller's music that well," I admitted.

"Everybody knows 'Moonlight Serenade!'" she said, and started to hum the song. Ruby had a beautiful voice. It was low and soulful. The tune got under my skin immediately. I recognized the song after all. Then she started snapping her fingers to "Chattanooga Choo Choo ." I had always loved that song. It was infectious in the way that it always reminded me of the clickety-clack of a train coming down the railroad tracks.

She sang softly so as not to wake Tammy.

"Sounds good, Ruby," said Dan from the driver's seat, tapping lightly on the steering wheel to keep in time. My fingers seemed to twitch with little beats of their own. The morphing seemed to be getting more intense as we approached Clarinda.

I had to fight the urge to pull my keyboard out from my backpack. We were approaching our destination. It was twilight when we got there. Everything was closed.

"There's a news briefing at 8 tomorrow morning," said Dan, reading an email from the police on his phone. "Let's walk around a little. I need to stretch my legs."

We got out of the car. I was anxious to check and see where Nathan's wallet had been found. Ruby wanted to show me the house where Glenn Miller had been born, where she'd played during the festival.

Tammy and Dan headed to the museum, but Ruby grabbed me by my arm so that I'd stay behind with her.

"Let's check it out," she said to me, motioning to a small house across a lawn. "We'll meet you guys in a few minutes." Tammy and Dan were already halfway across the lawn and barely noticed.

They seemed caught up in a father-daughter moment, which made me miss my own dad and again I regretted how bratty I'd been with him.

Ruby and I walked towards the house and she told me the story of how she first musi-morphed. It had happened right here at the birthplace of Glenn Miller.

She had done really well with her quartet, but the memory of it was overshadowed by sadness.

She had travelled to Clarinda with Daniel, her boyfriend. He had been her first serious boyfriend, her first true love.

Daniel was a brilliant oboe player. They had met during orchestra at school. He was in the quartet too. They had dated all throughout high school, but in those weeks leading up to the Glenn Miller festival, they had drifted apart.

Ruby never understood it completely. She was baffled by her own feelings. Maybe it was because Daniel was going to New York in the fall. He had been admitted to Julliard. It was fantastic. He clearly had a brilliant musical career ahead of him.

Ruby hadn't even tried to apply to Julliard. Besides, New York terrified her. She was a small town girl. She would be going to the University of Wisconsin to study music and business. Ruby had always been the more practical one of the two.

She wasn't as talented as Daniel. She didn't think so anyway. But having college looming in the fall had changed everything. They had barely spoken on the way to Clarinda. And then the whole thing with the necklace happened.

For her birthday, Daniel had given Ruby a gold necklace with a small gold flute charm. She had taken it off that week and then it had gone missing.

Daniel had gotten really upset with Ruby. Ruby had looked everywhere, but hadn't found it. They travelled to the festival with this wedge between them.

Their quartet performed quite well, though. The two other quartet members were their friends Lily, who played violin, and Justin, who played piano. They performed Bach and received a rousing applause from the judges.

"Do you want to come with me to get a drink?" Ruby asked Daniel as he folded up his music stand afterwards.

"No thanks. I'm good," he said. So Ruby left Daniel and wandered through the festival in search of a drink. When she came back he was gone. She wandered the grounds for an hour but couldn't find him. Feeling hurt, she finally took the shuttle back to the hotel. She went to her room but he wasn't there. So she knocked on her friend Lily's room. Ruby heard giggling inside.

She knocked again. Lily finally opened the door. Daniel stood behind Lily. Ruby felt like she'd been punched in the stomach when she saw the two of them together like that. How long had this been going on, she wondered bitterly? And Daniel had made her feel so guilty about the necklace. He wasn't such a saint himself.

"Ruby, it's not what you think! I'm sorry," he said, rushing up to her.

"I don't want to talk to you!" she said, backing away.

"You don't understand," he said. Ruby didn't want to hear his lame excuses. She turned and left.

"And that's the last time I saw Daniel," Ruby told me now as we neared the house.

"Didn't you go back to Wisconsin with him?" I asked.

"No. He and Lily were trying to tell me that he had decided to leave for Europe from there," she said. "Lily wound up meeting him there later that summer. I haven't spoken to him since that day. I don't even know where he lives."

Ruby said she went back to the festival that night by herself. She didn't know what else to do. She didn't want to hang around the hotel, knowing the two of them were together nearby.

And that's when it happened. She wound up morphing.

We had reached the house. I peeked through a window into an old-fashioned kitchen, with a four-legged stove and well-worn pots and pans hanging from nails on the wall. It was neat and spare.

"We performed on the lawn right here," said Ruby, waving to the yard by the house. "They set up bleachers and snack tables and all that kind of stuff," she said.

I tried to imagine Daniel and felt sorry for Ruby. That must've been so painful. This whole adventure was opening up something new in me. I felt myself growing musically, but something else was happening. I now really understood how one's heart could be broken. I'd always remember this as the summer of my first kiss. That was, if I made it out alive.

"I wound up changing my major to business instead of music. I dropped all of my music classes, in fact," said Ruby.

"That's horrible!" I exclaimed. "Especially after you won second place here," I said.

"It was just too painful. I was never as good as Daniel or Lily," she said.

"I think you're being modest," I said.

"You're a good player," Ruby said. How would she know that?

"I heard you playing in the hangar last night," she said, catching me off guard. Last night now seemed like years ago.

"But you were sleeping in the tent," I stammered.

"I couldn't sleep," she said, shaking her head. "I felt like seeing the hangar again. So I walked over there and I heard you playing 'American Pie.' It sounded great," she said, smiling.

"I morphed last night," I said. There was no turning back now. We both knew we were musiators. But all the color drained from Ruby's face.

"You did?" she gasped.

"Something also drew me to the hangar. And when I got there, I couldn't shake off the urge to play 'American Pie.' And then I morphed to the Surf Ballroom to The Day the Music Died," I said.

Ruby's hand flew over her mouth reflexively. "Was Nathan ... there?"

"I think he was. I felt him but I didn't see him," I said, staring into her eyes.

"But I helped him," I added gently.

"I knew he was alive," she cried, looking the happiest I'd ever seen her since the demo. "First he went to the Surf Ballroom and now he must be with Glenn Miller," she said, looking around with new appreciation. I nodded feeling so relieved that someone finally understood what was happening. Ruby totally got it. She pulled a flute from her bag.

"Maybe we can go there right now!" I couldn't believe she'd been carrying a flute around all this time. She said she'd given up music after Daniel, but apparently she had found her way back to the flute at some point.

"I found this in a thrift store recently. Something made me pick it up," she said shyly. And without another word she started playing a flawless, sinewy rendition of "Moonlight Serenade." She was great. I tapped my foot to the song. I pulled out my keyboard and fell right into the song with her. I played it as if I'd studied it for years, surprising even myself. Could we morph right here, right now?

It felt great to be making the music. But nothing unusual happened. After the song ended, Ruby put down her flute, looking disappointed.

"I guess the time's not right," I said.

"Let's try again," she said, lifting her flute and launched into another song. This time, I just wanted to enjoy listening to her. Dan and Tammy strolled over with smiles on their faces.

"Ruby. I didn't know you could play. You sound great!" said Tammy, looking at me. "I knew you two had a lot in common," she exclaimed. I smiled.

"Hate to break up the party, but we need to find a motel for the night," said Dan. Ruby finished the song and put her flute away.

"Nathan must enjoy hearing you play," said Tammy.

"He's never heard me," said Ruby. "We've always been so busy with flying," she said. "But if I ever see Nathan again, I'm going to make sure that music is part of our lives." She didn't know it, but she was echoing the same emotions that Nathan had felt earlier in Musicland.

I hoped silently to myself that I would be able to help make Ruby's dream come true. I packed my keyboard and took one last look around the grounds for now. I was anxious to see it all in the daytime, the house, the museum and the grounds.

We got back into the car and drove through downtown Clarinda. Dan said there was a motel up the road called the Glenn Miller Inn.

CHAPTER TWENTY-FIVE

Time to Time

A Channel 4 news truck rolled into the parking lot of the motel just as we were checking in.

"Ugh. I don't feel like talking with any reporters," grumbled Ruby. Through the window of the motel reception area, we saw two guys in the news truck.

The hotel clerk had recognized us the minute we walked in. "Ain't you the girlfriend of that missing pilot from Oshkosh?" said the woman. The receptionist had a badge that said Madge. She looked like a Madge to me. She wore her brown hair swept up in a beehive that accentuated her shining bright blue eyes and had a sizeable wattle under her chin.

"It's the craziest thing them finding his wallet out here. What do you make of that?" she asked, shaking her head in bewilderment. But then her mouth turned down in a little frown when she saw the troubled look on Ruby's face.

"Oh. I'm sorry hon," she said patting Ruby on the arm. "I'm sure they'll find him. They have that satellite stuff nowadays. He's got to show up. My nephew George is in the police academy and he said they've assigned every single Clarinda cop to this!"

She noticed Ruby and I glancing nervously out the window at the news truck.

"Those nosy bodies," she said to Ruby with a wink.

"They need something to run on the evening news. They don't care how they get it," said Ruby. And just then Madge made an executive decision. She opened a door leading to stairway behind her. The door had been marked "Employees Only" but Madge motioned to us to move quickly towards the stairs.

"You can go this way," she said, handing us hotel room card keys with a picture of the Glenn Miller Inn on it.

"I'm not supposed to let guests go up this way, but these are extenuating circumstances. The rooms are three flights up on your left. I'll stall these guys and give them rooms far away from yours," she said.

"Thanks!" I exclaimed as we scurried past her, climbing up the narrow flight of stairs. We got to the third floor and looked for our rooms. Ruby and I would share one room, and Tammy and her dad would take another.

"I'll run out and get some dinner. Why don't you guys all try to rest a little," said Dan in the hallway as Ruby and I found our room. "Zoey, please call your parents and tell them we're in Clarinda for the night. They can call me if they have any questions. Tell them we'll head back to Oshkosh right after the press briefing."

I had the feeling I would not be heading back to Oshkosh tomorrow. There was no use in arguing with Dan or my folks about that right now, though. So I just nodded as I slid the room key into our door. It was a clean, unexceptional motel room. I went over to one of the two beds and plopped down.

I could have easily fallen asleep but just then, my phone rang. It was Dad, speak of the devil.

"Hey Zoey. I heard the search party's now moved to Clarinda," he said, sounding formal.

"Yes," I said holding my breath. I had never really defied him like this before. Everything was new territory. We were still getting to know each other.

There was a pause. "I was expecting to see you by tonight."

"I know but this has taken on a life of its own." This was true but right at that moment I wished that I could just be back on tour with my father.

"Dan's driving back after the briefing tomorrow," I said.

"I heard," he said. The conversation felt strained. There was so much I wanted to say, but I couldn't think of where to begin. And then before I knew it, he was saying goodbye and I felt a wrenching in the pit of my stomach.

Life was complicated. After I hung up I just lay on my bed feeling drained. Ruby got up from the other bed where she had collapsed and looked at some of the wall art. The room was adorned with photos of Glenn Miller and World War II memorabilia. I recognized the photo of the Swing Kids that had been in my textbook.

"That's strange," I mumbled.

"What?"

"I have that same exact picture in my textbook," I said gesturing to the Swing Kids photo. Ruby stared at it a while and then moved to one of Miller in uniform.

I thought about Nathan. Was he with this man in the photo? I wished once again I could figure out how Zapallero had done it.

It had been odd how I'd gotten to the Surf Ballroom and the Stevie Ray concert right in the nick of time. I had been so busy that I hadn't had time to think about it until now. But suddenly the coincidence hit me.

How could I have landed in both these places at the same time these artists were set to fly? How had I done that? Or had someone done it to me? The last thought sent a wave of fear through me.

"We've got to get Nathan before he gets on Glenn Miller's plane," I said. "I did it before. I saved him from Buddy's and Stevie Ray's flights," I said. I didn't need to share my latest doubts with her.

"Let's try it again," said Ruby, pulling out her flute resolutely.

"Okay." I got my keyboard.

Ruby coaxed the first few lines of "Chattanooga Choo Choo" from her flute, sounding soulful and swingy. It was easy to accompany her.

As we played, I started picturing soldiers and ladies twirling on a dance floor circa 1944. The music felt great. It felt invigorating. I tried to picture Nathan together with Glenn Miller.

I visualized Miller's band practicing "Chattanooga Choo Choo" just like we were at that moment. It was eerie but it felt as if I was in the band that was in my mind's eye. I scanned the mental image for Nathan. I didn't see him. And then all of a sudden the room shook. Ruby and I glanced at each other.

The room shook again more forcefully. It was happening. The notes kept pouring out of Ruby's flute like sweet syrup. I felt totally connected musically to Ruby now. We were playing in sync. We were more than just two girls thrown together by horrible and bizarre circumstances.

We also shared this wonderful ability, this wonderful secret. The room vibrated even more violently. I was nearly thrown off the bed, but I held my ground and kept playing. And then it happened. The room lifted. I looked out the window and saw that we were airborne and sailing through the sky. I could see the motel now as we departed for this other world, leaving Clarinda in our wake.

Ruby played on, looking peaceful. There was a lot of hope riding on this, I thought as I glanced out the window. We were floating through something that resembled the Grand Canyon, but the colors were even more dramatic than the magnificent landmark in Arizona. Instead of light pinks and greens, the steep-sided canyon was embellished in bright blues, purples and hot pinks.

But then the sky grew darker and we heard a deep rumbling sound. Everything kept getting darker. The room rocked back and forth as it was pounded by a strong winds.

Ruby stopped playing. "What's happening?" she said, putting down her flute.

"Keep playing!" I urged. "I've been through this before," I added, and had another thought. "This is actually good," I said.

Ruby looked at me sceptically but resumed her playing.

"It's good because Glenn Miller was grounded for a few days by a terrible storm. Maybe we're flying through that storm right now, which would mean he hasn't taken off," I said.

Encouraged, Ruby picked up her instrument and began playing again.

We rode the storm for a while and then the room came to a halt. We kept playing for a few seconds before we realized we'd stopped moving.

"We're here," I said. We both stopped playing and the room became eerily quiet.

CHAPTER TWENTY-SIX

Ruby and Zoey's Road Trip

We glanced nervously at each other and then I got up and timidly walked over to the window. It was very dark outside, almost pitch black. The wind kept battering the sides of the room. Now I saw there were patches of snow covering the ground. This was going to be tricky, considering we were both dressed for summer.

"We'd better layer up as much as possible. Let's take those blankets," I said, my teeth chattering.

"Maybe we should go back. Can we go back please?" asked Ruby sounding terrified.

I shook my head. "You know it doesn't work that way. You can't go back until you've had a music lesson. And we're here to help Nathan. This may be our one and only chance." I looked into her eyes solemnly.

"Are you sure we can help him? How can we even find him? And what happens if he doesn't want to come home with me?"

"Nathan is not like Daniel. He loves you. And you've got to believe in yourself and your musicality more than ever, Ruby. It's very important, now more than ever. The music will bring you together. I truly believe that. Evil may have separated you but music will bring you together."

"Okay." She nodded but didn't look entirely convinced. She walked over to her overnight bag and pulled out some shirts and started layering up.

I did the same. Neither of us had a proper winter jacket, but with several layers and blankets draped over our shoulders, it seemed like we'd be able to tough out the bitter cold outside. But when I opened the door, a chilling wind blasted me from head to toe and my layers felt like paper.

I didn't have time to reconsider, however, because the wind knocked us off our feet and we began to slide on our backsides down an icy hill.

We landed on top of each other at the muddy bottom of the hill. My spirit was sinking quickly but then I heard something familiar and welcoming. It was Amadeus.

"Zoey! Ruby! Thank God you made it here!" he said in his nasally British accent as he parted icy bushes to greet us.

"You know Ruby?"

"I know everybody who comes to Musicland," said the squirrel, irritated. "But there's no time for small talk. The world's at war and one of our greatest band leaders is about to fly into a horrible storm! Your friend Nathan has been hired to fly Glenn Miller!"

"Is Nathan okay?" blurted Ruby

"Yes. He's fine and an incredibly gifted clarinet player," said the squirrel.

"I still can't believe I didn't know that," said Ruby. I too was baffled at how these two gifted musicians had managed to hide their talents from each other.

"Let's hurry," said Amadeus and he started sprinting through the snowy woods. We followed him. Music was playing in the distance. It grew louder. I started to recognize strands of Glenn Miller's music. We came to a stream and trekked over icy and slippery rocks to cross it.

"You okay, Ruby?" I asked. I heard her struggling a few feet behind.

"I'm good," she said.

Amadeus deftly hopped from rock to rock without any trouble.

"We're getting closer," he said.

We heard the band loud and clear now. We were only a few hundred feet away when the rain came. This was the final straw. I lost my balance. I fell into the icy creek, coating myself with mud. I wanted to cry but knew that wouldn't do anybody any good. I got myself up and kept going.

Ruby fell more than once. I tried to help her and then she pulled me down with her. We were soaked, muddy, chilled and miserable.

But we pulled ourselves up and approached a building that was lit up inside. The orchestra inside sounded amazing.

"We made it!" I gasped, wiping water from my eyes. I wasn't sure if it was tears or rain. Through a window, I saw a swing band made up of animals and people dressed in 1940s army uniforms. I scanned the group nervously for Nathan, but didn't see him.

"So this is where the orchestra practiced. They were trying to record a whole bunch of shows before they went to France. Miller planned to go ahead of the band to set things up," said Amadeus sadly.

"But he never made it," I said, grimly finishing his thought.

"Correct," said Amadeus, but then tilted his head cockeyed as he seemed to have a sudden thought. He checked the tiny watch he wore on his tiny wrist.

"It is December 14, the day before Miller's flight," he said matter-of-factly.

Ruby and I looked at each other. We both realized we needed to get in there and find Nathan and stop him before he got on Glenn Miller's plane.

"Let's go," said Amadeus at the door to the building. "Its freezing out here and the music is just so irresistible," he said.

I grabbed him by his little parka. "I don't see Nathan," I said, staring intensely in his eyes. I said it low so that Ruby couldn't hear me. She was looking through the window with hope in her eyes.

Amadeus was surprised at my boldness. He was usually the one giving the orders.

"He was here a few minutes ago," he said quietly.

"You lied! You said he was here! I've got to find him, Amadeus. I can't keep missing him," I spat.

Amadeus looked nervously at Ruby, who was now regarding us both suspiciously.

"He was here a few minutes ago," he repeated. "I would never lie. This just keeps happening," said Amadeus.

"What keeps happening?" said Ruby with a little screech in her voice. She was looking very strained.

"Tony Zapallero is one step ahead of us," I said.

"Right," said Amadeus.

"We've got to find Nathan!" shrieked Ruby, wiggling the door knob. It was locked.

"Have you met Zaparello?" I asked.

My furry friend nodded. "He came here in search of his mother. But his search turned cold because he didn't believe enough in his own talents. He never found his mother, but found other ways to use his powers. And he's very dangerous. He was banned from Musicland long ago," said Amadeus.

"But he knows how to send others in and out at will," I said.

"Yes," said Amadeus.

Ruby started rattling the doorknob again.

"Stay calm Ruby," I said. "It won't help to get hysterical. We're no good to Nathan that way," I said and suddenly the door opened for Ruby.

She ran in and we raced after her. We entered the big room where the band was playing. We were quite a sight, two young females from the future, caked in mud, wearing blankets draped around our shoulders like hobos.

We searched the band in hopes of finding Nathan. But of course he was not there. The rehearsal had just ended.

Everyone in the band was packing up their instruments. Glenn Miller really wasn't Glenn Miller, but a kangaroo with thick horn-rimmed glasses like the real bandleader.

"Keep up the good work guys," he said to the musicians. "I'll see you all soon in France."

I strode up to him since I had nothing to lose at this point. "Excuse me sir. Have you seen a young pilot named Nathan here?"

The kangaroo looked at me curiously but before he had a chance to answer I heard a familiar voice from the back of the room say, "He's gone."

I scanned the room in search of that voice. I knew it. I'd heard it somewhere before. Ruby recognized it too. We studied the band members again. Far in the back row of the string players sat an older man. He had white hair and wore an air force uniform. I knew who it was instantly. It was John Kiefer.

CHAPTER TWENTY-SEVEN

Up and Down

"Where's Nathan?" shrieked Ruby, running up to Kiefer. She couldn't contain herself any longer.

"You just missed him. He was redeployed," said Kiefer. I looked at the Cougar executive, disliking him more with each second.

It was all that Ruby could take. She wilted as the adrenaline that had kept her going through the miserable hike seeped out of her like air from a balloon.

Reflexively, I put my arm around Ruby to steady her, glaring at Kiefer.

I was disappointed but also kicked myself for being surprised. Had I really expected this to be so easy? Zap had been one step ahead of us all the way. I felt Nathan's presence here even though he was gone. It would have been sweet to see him scoop Ruby in his arms, like he had in the hangar that day. I squeezed my eyes to stop from crying.

I studied Kiefer's face. He looked haggard and had stubble on his chin. He actually looked pretty terrible. "What are you doing here?" I asked icily, but felt myself thaw a little as I read a deep sadness in Kiefer's eyes.

"I couldn't let him do it," he said.

"What?" I challenged.

"Fly. I couldn't let Nathan fly Glenn Miller. It's all Zapallero's doing, but I'm responsible as well," he said.

"How does he do it? How does he send Nathan to these exact places and times? " I asked.

"He programs it. He's doing it to you too. How else do you think you keep winding up in these spots?" exclaimed Kiefer.

"Oh my God," gasped Ruby.

I felt a little faint at the thought. So I was being "programmed," after all. I thought I was getting the places to save Nathan, but Zap had been actually bringing me. I had probably been programmed to follow the same itinerary as Nathan. Zapallero was trying to kill me the same way he was trying to kill Nathan. But somehow, we had both survived.

"Where's Nathan heading now? What's his new assignment with the Air Force? Where has Zapallero sent him?" I asked.

"Zap didn't send him anywhere. He doesn't even know I'm here," said Kiefer.

Ruby and I looked at each other in disbelief. "Why didn't you send him home?" I demanded.

"Not that simple," said Kiefer. "Zapallero has locked Nathan into Europe during the war. I wanted to distance

Nathan from Glenn Miller, but he was convinced he could get himself home if he could get into a plane. He's gone with a few other men for airborne training. I got him to agree to this new assignment," said Kiefer, but then added, "I don't know how strong my powers are against Zapallero. Nathan's still in great danger. I'm sorry." He looked forlorn.

Even though I hated him for being weak against Zap, I pitied him too.

"Nathan had never even listened to this music before," he continued. "Even after I told him what happened to Glenn Miller, Nathan was reluctant to abandon the mission. He thought he could change the course of history," he said sadly. "But you know that's not how it works. History replays itself here."

I nodded. I too had learned the hard way that you can't change history in Musicland. "If Zapallero fixed him to fly Buddy Holly, Stevie Ray and Glenn Miller, he can do it again," I said.

Kiefer nodded. "Yes. Or he may realize we're on to him and try something new."

"What do you mean?" I asked, not liking the sound of this. Even though this had been a deadly game of cat and mouse, I had at least figured out Zapallero's method to his madness. If he stopped sending Nathan to musical air disasters, I had no idea what to expect.

"He's got him in a very volatile region during a very dark time in history," said Kiefer. "Look into the Swing Kids," he said.

"Swing Kids," I repeated. I knew I'd heard that term before and recalled reading about the Swing Kids in Anna's textbook.

"Tell me more. You have to help us," I exclaimed.

Kiefer smiled sadly. "I'm afraid I've come to the end of this mission. I've volunteered to fly in Nathan's place," he said. He had the look of someone who wanted to die.

"Can't any of these other guys fly?" I asked, motioning towards the band members.

"No," he said. He seemed resolved, almost relieved. Poor Kiefer had lost his will to live. He was one of those lost souls that Mrs. B had once told me about.

I recalled the time I had musi-morphed onto the deck of the Titanic and had thought I would die. It had been the saddest day of my life.

I'd managed to barely survive and had witnessed more death than anyone should ever see in a lifetime. Mrs. B told me afterwards that it was possible to lose yourself forever in Musicland. Some people never returned.

There was always that risk when you went there, especially if you'd stopped believing in your music. You could get trapped in the event. It was rare but it did happen.

And it happened most frequently with people who wanted to die.

Mrs. B said some people never found their muse in Musicland. Instead, they found truths that were so painful that they made the person want to end it all.

Musicland was likely their last stop on a long, sad journey. Throughout history, many artists, musicians, composers have taken their lives. Many have been found dead in their homes, leaving suicide notes. There were always a few of these tortured but brilliant artists who took their lives every generation.

But what people didn't realize is that they morphed back one last time in search of something. I felt sad about Kiefer. I got the sense he might be on this kind of mission right now.

"You don't have to get on that plane," I said softly. "We need you. You're the only one who really knows how Zapallero operates. This isn't just about Nathan. We need to squash Zapellero once and for all."

Kiefer shook his head. "I'd be no help. I'd only bring you harm. He's got me. Tomorrow I'll fly Glenn Miller across the channel. Someone in Musicland has to do it and that someone is me."

I looked down as I felt a tugging on my sleeve. Amadeus was now standing between Kiefer and I. "We must go. It's time," said the squirrel. I could see that Kiefer couldn't be convinced, and we had little time to waste.

"Good bye," I said, never expecting to see him again. I followed Amadeus. When I looked back Kiefer was as pale as a ghost.

CHAPTER TWENTY-EIGHT

Master Lesson

Amadeus, Ruby and I found ourselves moments later walking down the dimly lit cave hallway to Mrs. B's place. I was thinking about what Kiefer said. What had he meant about the Swing Kids? Ruby walked quietly behind me. I worried about her too, but she seemed to be holding up pretty well under the circumstances.

Amadeus rapped his little fist on Mrs. B's door and it swung open. Mrs. B. hugged me as she had the last time. Again, it gave me great comfort.

Then she stepped back, studying my face and keeping her hand on my shoulder. "You've had some close calls but your music has steered you through." She gently let go and looked past me into Ruby's eyes.

"Look at you! It's been such a long time," she said softly and then she and Ruby were hugging. Ruby was smiling and crying at the same time.

"I'm glad to see you both safe and sound. Follow me," said the mammoth woman, leading us into her apartment to the room with rugs on the walls. We sat at the little table as Mrs. B left the room. She returned within seconds carrying a tray of steaming tea and cookies. I was feeling much better now. I poured tea for Ruby and myself and settled back into the plump, comfy cushion of my chair.

"Do you know where Nathan is?" Ruby asked after sipping her tea.

Mrs. B frowned. It was unusual to see her downbeat. "He's still here in Musicland, but I'm not sure where. Nathan's morphed again."

"I keep missing him by seconds," I said.

"I know. But this time it was because John Kiefer stepped in," Mrs B said mysteriously.

"I asked him to join us, but he was so ....resigned to dying," I said feeling sad again. "Why is that? I don't understand how all this is happening?" I hoped Mrs B had some answers.

"We have a very precarious situation on our hands," she said, shaking her head.

I didn't feel my usual sense of reassurance from her right now. "Will Kiefer really just vanish now and forever?"

Mrs B smiled a little now. "No. I think John Kiefer would have preferred that, but Zapallero has already morphed him out of Glenn Miller's plane. Tony Zapallero apparently had other plans for John Kiefer."

I was glad to hear Kiefer was alive, although I cringed when I imagined where Zapallero may have sent him.

"Kiefer said that we should look into the swing kids. Do you know what he was talking about?"

Mrs. B looked alarmed. "His power is growing, Zoey," said Mrs. B. "If you know history, you know the atrocities inflicted by the Nazis."

I nodded solemnly.

"You really need to stop him. He keeps sending people to the most sorrowful moments in history, when death silenced music. Just think about all the sad flights you've witnessed over the past few hours," she said. "That's not a coincidence. I'm afraid he's gotten on to you, kid. And you're the only one with the power to stop him. If you don't I'm afraid he'll kill you. He'll kill us all and turn Musicland into Deathland!" She burst into sobs.

I'd never ever seen Mrs. B so distressed. It terrified me. She'd been my rock here in Musicland. Ice cold fear gripped me from head to toe. Why was this happening? Where in the world was Nathan? I just wanted to go back to Los Angeles and high school and be a normal kid. I didn't want to save Musicland. I didn't want to take on this monster. I didn't want to die.

CHAPTER TWENTY-NINE

Swing time for Nazis

I would soon learn that Nathan made it only as far as the first round of airborne training drills in his new deployment before he was morphed again by Zapallero. This time Zap sent him a few hundred miles across Europe to Nazi Germany.

Nathan's spirit was sinking. He didn't know how much more he could endure after living through the greatness and then the demise of Buddy Holly, Stevie Ray and Glenn Miller.

He felt he must be nearing death himself. Each time he thought he was getting closer to home, he realized tragedy was right around the bend. But even such thoughts couldn't prepare for him for his next destination.

Never in his dreams could he have imagined that he would witness such torture. Nathan had landed in a place where soldiers were being trained to kill innocents. It was also a place where music in many forms was strictly forbidden.

Zapallero had sent him to Germany when the ruling Nazis set out to execute millions of Jews and Gypsies and other people they deemed impure. The Nazis also set out to eliminate jazz and other art they considered unworthy of the country's Aryan race.

At first Nathan thought he was at a typical 1940s American dance party. Well, it was as typical as you could get with the floor populated by people and those musical animal creatures native to Musicland. He didn't realize he was actually at a party thrown by Swing Kids, the German underground youth jazz movement.

Like me, Nathan had also read about the Swing Kids. He knew that many had been arrested and deported to concentration camps.

Nathan had morphed back to August 1944 into one of the most brutal German police operations against Swing Kids in history. Over 300 kids were arrested.

Jazz was particularly loathed by the Nazis not only because it was American but because it was enjoyed and performed by blacks and Jews in particular.

It was hard for Nathan at first to understand that he was in any danger as he stood in the middle of the dance floor. A young girl, sporting an American-looking ponytail and skirt walked up to him. "Hi," she said in English but with a thick German accent.

Despite the Nazi efforts, jazz flourished under their rule as these rebellious teens took to it with a vengeance. The SS discouraged all but the dull rap tap national music employed in most propaganda material. But these kids defied that by secretly throwing parties and smuggling in jazz records.

As the war dragged on, the Nazis got more and more infuriated. One German Swing Kid was shot at one of the swing parties. Nathan was surprised at the girl's accent because she looked so American.

But then he looked around and realized everyone was speaking German. The band started playing a Glenn Miller tune and he felt the swing tempo sweep through his veins.

The girl took his hand. He had no problem dancing with her. It felt good and the pretty girl reminded him a little of Ruby. Nathan missed her, wondering if he'd ever feel her in his arms again. He wondered how she was coping and what it must have been like for her that day in Oshkosh, when his plane disappeared. It was all a big blur to him.

As his body swayed to the satiny big band music, he vowed yet again to work on his clarinet playing for the rest of his life if he made it back alive. He hoped he'd be able to share this part of himself with Ruby.

And just then, Nathan got a strong conviction. He knew right then that his life actually depended on music. Music was his salvation. Music would get him out of this mess, he thought, looking at all the swing kids.

"Are you from here?" asked a handsome young man dancing next to him. He also spoke English with a thick German accent. Nathan shook his head.

"I'm a long way from home," he replied.

"I thought so. Sally, give the guy a break," said the young German affectionately to the girl Nathan was dancing with. "I think this poor fellow needs a drink!"

"Sorry," said the girl in English, blushing.

"It's okay," Nathan said.

They stopped dancing and the girl led Nathan to a table and motioned for him to sit. In a matter of seconds, she was handing him a glass of ice water. Nathan took a deep swig. It tasted wonderful.

"We hold these dances whenever we can, but it's getting more difficult. I'm Otto," said the young man extending his hand. Nathan shook it.

"The Nazis are onto us. They busted up a party two weeks ago and carted off some kids to the camps," Otto said.

Nathan casually withdrew his hand as fear began to creep through his bones. He looked around the room with new eyes and an uneasy feeling as he realized he was at a Swing Kids party. He saw how these kids emulated American styles with trench coats, fedoras, zoot suits, tight dresses and sweaters. He remembered reading how many of these kids had refused to participate in Hitler's Nazi Youth program.

Nathan was in Hamburg, which had been the center of the movement. It was where Hitler took his most brutal action against these kids. Nathan felt more and more nervous as he watched the kids laughing and dancing around him. And then his worst fears came true when the music was suddenly drowned out by wailing sirens.

"Hurry, let's get out of here," cried Otto, pushing Nathan towards the exit.

But it was too late. By the time they got there, the doorway was blocked by menacing SS Soldiers.

"Swing heil!" said Otto defiantly using the Swing Youth's popular way of saying hello. He directed it to a giant of an SS officer, who was bearing down on them.

"What did you say?" asked the officer with a creepy smile.

Nathan froze, swallowing hard. His muscles tightened.

"Run!" whispered Otto in his ear but it was no use as the officer struck Otto hard in the face with a billy club. Nathan heard the sickening sound of Otto's nose cracking and saw blood spurting down his face.

Nathan felt like he might faint as he and other kids were pushed roughly to the ground.

"This is a mistake. I'm American!" screamed Nathan, but his words were muted as he put his arms around his face to protect himself from hard kicks.

Soldiers, some of them actually wolves in uniforms, stood all around the kids laughing with terrifying glee. "Some good hard work in a camp will set you straight from wanting to be like the Americans," said the soldier who had broken Otto's nose. He was now pinning Nathan down on the floor and held a rock-like fist against Nathan's forehead.

From the corner of his eye, Nathan could see Otto lying on the ground next to him, staring unemotionally at a soldier who had his foot placed squarely on his neck.

Nathan would later learn that Otto was half-Jewish, which surely meant death for him. Being a Swing Kid was risky enough but downright fatal if the kid also happened to be a Jew. Nathan looked around and saw blood everywhere as SS officers beat up kids using sticks and hands and boots.

Sally, the young girl he'd just danced with, struggled between two officers who pinned her arms behind her back.

Not long ago, Nathan had been blissfully playing clarinet in Glenn Miller's big band. How had he wound up here? How would he survive this latest cruel twist of fate?

Nathan just wanted to stop the merry-go-round. But he knew that would not be easy as he felt himself being hauled up from the ground by two soldiers. They pushed him along with many others through a door leading outside the ballroom.

"Where are they taking us?" whispered Nathan to Otto, who was moving beside him in the crowd still bleeding from his nose. His eyes had already started to swell shut, leaving just slits.

"The camps," said Otto grimly.

This couldn't be happening, insisted Nathan silently as he summoned all of his strength and courage. Without a word, he suddenly launched himself hard against the monstrous Nazi officer, who spun around and lunged, planting a hard kick into the barrel of Nathan's chest.

Nathan landed with a thud on the ground. His head exploded in pain and his neck snapped back as the soldier kicked him now in the face. The pain was blinding and he tasted blood in his mouth.

He staggered up, searching for an escape but was grabbed firmly by two more steel-armed soldiers. One of the Nazis leaned menacingly into his face. Nathan could smell his cologne mixed with sweat as he breathed heavily. "Don't try anything like that again," he sneered, then pushed Nathan back in line with the others. Nathan fought the urge to throw up as he was led with the others out of the room. There was no escaping now.

CHAPTER THIRTY

The Power of Music

R uby and I were still sitting in Mrs B's studio. But my mind was elsewhere. I had drifted off. I had heard Glenn Miller but had seen flashes of red and felt a terrible sense of foreboding. I looked at Mrs. B's mouth moving but didn't hear what she was saying. I willed myself to stay focused.

"Be strong," she said, patting my hand. "Do you remember what I told you that first time?"

I nodded. I would never forget that. She had said the same thing over and over and over again until the words would forever be imprinted in my brain.

She'd kept saying: "Music is good for you. Music is good for you. Music is good for you." The words had put me in a trance. And the next thing I remembered was waking up in the practice room at Harlan University, my life forever changed.

Mrs. B looked at me as if she could read my mind.

"You've come a long way, Zoey. But now you're on another journey. There is more for you to learn in terms of your own musicality, your own powers. You search for the answers from Musicland and it replies. Remember, music is good for you," she said.

"You may not always understand the answers but they reside in the depth of your soul. When the time is right, these answers will resurface and sing out from your heart."

"But how can I save Musicland? Zapallero seems so powerful," I asked, still not getting it.

"Will I ever see Nathan again?" Ruby piped in.

Mrs. B's face grew dark again, making me nervous. I hated to see Mrs. B show any doubt.

"Zapallero has created many imbalances. No one should ever enter Musicland through a portal other than their own. It's extremely dangerous for any of us who are already inside. It's up to you to close all those doors now," she said, staring into my eyes.

Why me, I wondered, thinking of how I'd enjoyed my life over the past three years, just being a regular teenager who liked to play piano.

I wanted to go back to that life. Meeting Joe had also opened up a whole new set of possibilities. I wanted out of this war between good and evil. It wasn't fair.

I wanted to be home with my parents, like other kids. I had never even had the chance to have both of them together under the same roof. We were going to try that in the fall. And now I might not even be around for it, I thought, pitying myself.

My father was expecting me to join him soon. How could I?

"Zoey. I am so proud of you," said Mrs. B. "And you too Ruby. I can't believe how far you've both come. Hearing you play so beautifully was so powerful, so good," she said. "I never expected anything like this could or would happen."

Ruby and I stirred uncomfortably. "All of us in Musicland are being tested," she said, waving her arm to illustrate her point. I couldn't touch my tea all of a sudden.

"Zoey. There's something I couldn't tell you before, but now it's time. I had hoped to prepare you for this, but the circumstances with Zapallero. Well, they're putting everything on a fast track," she said.

I searched her face as she glanced around nervously to see if anyone beside Ruby and I could hear her. I had never ever seen Mrs. B so paranoid.

"You have extraordinary musical power," she said to me. "Just the little time you've spent on ear training and blues shows how quick a study you are. You are special."

I nodded, encouraging her to proceed but nervous to hear what she had to say.

"Before you go, I just want to tell you one more thing. And after I tell you this, it will all make sense," she said, gearing herself up to continue.

"There's a connection between you and Tony Zapallero," she said.

My jaw dropped. What did she mean by a connection? I'd never met the greasy goon before I laid eyes on him at Oshkosh a couple of days ago.

"Tony Zapallero wasn't always rich and powerful. His father was, but he gave his son nothing. Tony had a hard childhood. His father was cruel. He abused him, musically."

"Abused him musically?" I had never heard of such a thing.

"It's very serious," said Mrs. B. "He forced him to play piano at age three and punished him severely if he didn't practice, locking him in the family's music studio for hours," she said.

I tried to fight any feelings of sympathy for Zapallero although I had to admit his childhood did sound kind of rough.

"Turns out Tony became quite good on the keyboard and even went on to study at Julliard," Mrs. B continued.

Ruby jumped when she heard Julliard because it reminded her of Daniel.

"Tony Zapallero was so gifted, he became the youngest pianist to join the Chicago Philharmonic. But all the while he was a bitter person," the older woman said.

"Tony's mother was of no help. She was a beautiful violinist in her own right but an utterly weak and passive person. By doing nothing to stop her husband from torturing Tony, she was complicit in the act herself," Mrs B said, wiping away a tear.

She told us how Tony's mother had died in the family's music studio and the death was ruled a suicide. Tony's mother was one of those lost souls who morphed to Musicland one last time before she took her own life. She morphed back to the 1906 San Francisco earthquake and lost her life while playing violin in a small theatre.

"Tony came here looking for his mother but he never did find her. There are many ways to explain this and it has mostly to do with Tony, himself. But he blamed his father and set out to undo Musicland," she said.

"Zapallero broke the code of silence and began recruiting scientists to help him in his crusade to program people's musical DNA," she said, close to sobbing again.

I turned to face her to make sure if I was hearing this right. "Did you say he can program people's musical DNA?" I asked. "I didn't even know that people had musical DNA."

"Yes, they do. Zapallero steeped himself in a growing field of science involving music and the brain. Researchers believe that people carry genes that influence how they react to music. While music is regarded as the universal language that can evoke reactions from people across all cultural boundaries, more and more research is being devoted to study how human beings actually react uniquely to songs."

She told us how Tony had broken many rules as he hired scientists to try out his different theories. He'd paid them off to stay quiet. He started using his research to send animals here first and succeeded in greatly compromising Musicland. In the past few years, he'd spent much of his time using what he learned to manipulate these scientists to keep them under his control.

He even started sending these scientists in and out of Musicland. "He had been exiled but that didn't stop him from sending others there. And then there was the matter of his own father's rather strange death," she said, looking from Ruby to me.

I glanced at Ruby, who had turned a light shade of green.

"How did he die?" Ruby asked quietly.

"He died in a terrible car accident. He was driving in New York City when a huge piano van, carrying a grand piano with a price tag of $64,000, came barrelling through a red light and decapitated him."

I fought the urge to barf.

"Tony Zapallero's very powerful," added Mrs B for further emphasis.

I collapsed back into my chair, trying to process this. "Where was Tony when this accident happened?" I asked.

"He was in Massachusetts in his music lab. Nothing's ever been proven, but folks here in Musicland suspected Tony used his scientifically-enhanced musi-morphing powers to finish off his father."

Mrs. B let these words sink in now. "And it seems he's at it again with your friend Nathan Gordon," she said. "It's never been proven, but we know he can use his musical powers to move people and objects and he can direct them to specific destinations," she said sadly.

"And this is where you come in," she said, pointing her gaze at me.

"Me? What can I do?" I suddenly didn't care what happened to me anymore as long as I could bring back Nathan and get rid of this slime ball once and for all.

"You're as powerful as Zapallero," she said and then proceeded to tell me how my and Tony Zapallero's lives were connected.

CHAPTER THIRTY-ONE

On a Scale

Zapallero displayed signs of musical genius when he was very young, but then branched out in other ways as he got older. After a while, he abandoned music altogether to take up physics.

He went back to school to earn a second degree in robotics, enrolling at MIT with other rocket scientists. Many of his fellow students went on to start some of the biggest computer and technology companies in the world. Zapallero worked for a software outlet in New Hampshire after graduation but soon got bored and moved back to Boston to form his own company, Amtron.

As the company chief, Zapallero's mean side soon came through. "You jerk! Why aren't you doing this? What's the reason for this?" he'd yell at whoever was near, throwing pads, half-filled coffee cups or whatever was in his hand. "Moron! What am I paying you for?" His poor unfortunate workers would wipe the coffee from their clothes without a word.

What a jerk, I thought as I listened to Mrs. B describe him.

"But people put up with Tony Zapallero because he was always right," she said. "The other reason they put up with him was because Zapallero was perfecting his hypno-musimorphing skills and brainwashing everybody," she said.

I leaned back in my chair. "Oh my God," I said.

"Yes, not a good situation. Although everybody was also so happy with the generous dividends the company was paying off each month, they had no idea what was really being done to them," she said.

After a while people started to take note of Zapallero for the key advances his company made, but then he sold the firm and went underground again.

He was only twenty-eight and rich. He had sold Amtron for fifty million dollars, giving him a sizeable fortune. He bought a Cadillac and headed west to figure out his next move. But he only got as far as Indiana. It is there where Tony Zapallero met a girl and fell in love. Her name was Dana.

The name sounded vaguely familiar to me.

"The only problem with Dana was that she had a kid," continued my music teacher. "It was a drag, but Zapallero couldn't stay away from this beautiful, free-spirited country girl with big city dreams. He knew she was nobody, not worthy of someone like himself, but Zap just lost his head for a while," she said.

I tried to picture a younger version of the slicked-back mogul I met falling hard for a girl in the sticks. It didn't really compute.

"She was a hick but she was talented. She had a voice. Maybe she was a little like his mother. Zapallero loved her but he never really planned on committing. He never told her how rich he was and she didn't seem to care. Maybe that's why he loved her, but he also thought she was clueless and after a while, he lost all respect for her."

I was not surprised based on what I already knew about Zapallero.

"He told her he had been laid off from an engineering job in Chicago and was looking for work. He said he wanted a simpler life, away from the big city," said Mrs. B, putting her hand on mine. "Those were the happiest months of Tony Zapallero's life."

"What happened?" I asked.

"He moved in and played house for a while," she said, squeezing my hand. "It was nice for a few months, but then Zapallero grew restless. Dana and the kid started to irritate him. He bought the kid a guitar one day. He was only three, the same age that Zapallero had been when his father had force-fed him the piano."

"What a jerk," I muttered. "It's sad to see how history repeats itself." I felt bad for the little kid in this story in the same way I had felt bad for Zapallero when I'd heard about his youth.

Nodding and patting my hand again, Mrs. B continued. "To Zap's amazement, young Paul picked up the guitar like he'd been playing forever."

"How did Zap do that?" I asked.

"Zap didn't do a thing. The kid was authentic. He was very gifted," said Mrs. B. "But Zapallero got a brainstorm as he watched this young prodigy. He realized he had the perfect lab rat.

"Everything made sense all of a sudden," said Mrs. B. "Zapallero now realized why he had been drawn to this little hole in the wall. He was over Dana by now. She had grown too needy and clingy but he stayed a few more months and set up a lab in the basement. He made the kid Paul promise not to tell his mother anything because it was going to be a big surprise."

I felt uncomfortable listening to how Zapallero conducted his experiments on the poor little kid in that basement as he investigated the interaction of remote parts of the brain with musical sound.

He hooked the tyke up to an MRI and made him sing and play guitar. The monitor showed incredible imagery, nothing Zapallero or anyone had ever seen before. Zapallero discovered a chasm in the brain tissue that responds actively to music. This area of the brain was considered non-active according to most medical journals.

As far as he knew this was unchartered territory. He had mapped out others' "musical DNA" at Amtron while they were brainwashed but he had never seen a brain as musically advanced as Paul's. It was extraordinary. Paul's musical brain patterns were morphing with a liquidity that was hypnotizing.

In that basement, Zapallero developed the theory that would set the stage for his ultimate control of the world. He realized he could harness this obscure brain activity and use it for time travel. Zapallero discovered that if he synchronized the brain's movement with musical patterns and then held the player and the music beyond the pause sign in a written song, he could create a wormhole in time.

For instance, if Paul was playing "Happy Birthday" and Zap hypnotized him to stay on the pause longer than what was written on the sheet, Paul would be sucked through the pause sign to another time when that exact same song was being played.

Zapallero knew this kid was special, but if he perfected his skills, he could pull this off with others. He stayed with Paul and Dana for a few months, but then he knew it was time to move on. He was sick of playing house and sick of Dana, who was not half as talented or interesting as her son. So just like that, Tony Zapallero threw a few hundred dollar bills on the bed and left them without a word.

When Paul woke up that morning to hear his mother crying, he realized something was wrong. He ran down to the basement. Everything had been cleaned up. Tony had lied. He had said they were working on a surprise for his mom. He let out a wail and cried for hours.

He already missed the man who had seemed like a father and had set up the fun play area in the basement.

Dana finally shut him in his room without dinner and didn't come back to him for twelve hours. The next day, dazed and ghostlike, Dana packed up their few belongings and got on a bus with Paul for New York City. She was convinced Zapallero was there.

But she never found him. She went out with many other men, often leaving Paul alone in the apartment. And then one day she told him they were going back to Indiana.

Paul was so happy. He'd be back in the smaller town near his grandma.

Dana took him to Port Authority and walked him to a bus. She gave him his ticket.

"Go on and get a seat and don't get up," she said. So Paul walked on and sat down. Paul sat and waited for a long time and as the bus pulled away, he realized his mother wasn't coming. He ran to the bus window to look for her. But she was gone. He'd never see her again.

His grandmother was too old and sick to take care of him, so Paul moved from foster home to foster home in Indiana. He had a hard life. But he always had his music. He'd think about those times in the basement with Tony.

He knew Zap had done things that were wrong, played with his mind. But he had also made him feel special. Nobody had ever made a fuss about him like he had. Tony had given him that much. He'd made Paul feel talented.

I nodded, fascinated by the story, but was unprepared for what she said next.

"Zoey. That young boy was your dad," she blurted. "Tony Zapallero based his original 'experiment' on your father's DNA. This is why you have the power to beat him at his own game. Your DNA is the source of Zapallero's prototype!" she said.

I sat back as the words sunk in. This explained everything. Now I knew why she believed I had the power to save Musicland. It was all because of my dad.

And I had inherited his genes, along with a huge responsibility.

"Oh my God!" gasped Ruby.

"It's all about the music," said Mrs. B with a sad smile. "With each journey here, you grow stronger musically. We need your help, Zoey. You are different. You're special. You are the one who can find Nathan and bring him back," she said.

CHAPTER THIRTY-TWO

Night Music

At the very moment that I was learning about how Zapallero had impacted my life, my friend Nathan was sitting with hundreds of lost souls packed like cattle in a dark train heading to a concentration camp. He was still in Germany in 1944 because of that crazy man.

Had it really been just yesterday when he was soaring above Oshkosh feeling like he was on top of the world? Nathan had been doing what he loved most: flying. But now he was on a train heading towards unthinkable horrors.

How had this happened? He'd been in the Silo when he suddenly heard music. It had been odd because he hadn't turned on the radio. It was coming from outside but then it grew louder, as if it was playing inside, and soon drowned out everything. It grew so loud it made it impossible for him to focus on flying.

The song was Buddy Holly's, "That'll Be the Day." Nathan was a huge Holly fan but had found it eerie to hear that particular song right then. And then everything went purple and he had found himself in a funky musical world with people and musical animals.

It had been scary and spectacular. Through it all, he had wanted to go home, but now he wasn't sure he was going to make it. Someone was out to get him, Nathan thought sadly as the train sped quickly through the night.

He prayed for another song. Couldn't music take him out of here? People were standing. The SS, the terrifying soldiers of the Nazi Party, had ordered everyone to stand, not sit. That had been hours ago. There were no soldiers in the car and there hadn't been since they left and slammed the door shut, leaving the prisoners in darkness.

Everyone sat at some point, praying there would be enough time to stand up once the soldiers unbolted the door. This was a game to the soldiers. They liked to catch a few sitting each time. And then they'd shoot them.

Nathan despairingly recalled what he had learned about the Holocaust in college. The train stopped. Everyone sprang to their feet. The door opened and a cruel-looking soldier walked in. He looked disappointed he hadn't caught anyone sitting.

"Give me all your gold pieces and other valuables now!" he barked. "Those who don't will be shot! And if anyone tries to escape, you are all dead," he spat and then left. The doors clanked shut behind him. Several people gasped in relief.

Nathan travelled in the car for two more days. Finally, it stopped and a young boy yelled as he peeked through a crack in the door.

"I see a camp!" he exclaimed. Nathan scrambled towards the crack. He saw a courtyard surrounded by a barbed wire wall with a watch tower. His heart beat fast. Was there a way out of this predicament?

He smelled something putrid and knew what it was. He had read about the giant ovens they gassed people in. A thick black ribbon of smoke rose from a chimney in a building next to the watch tower. Was that oven waiting for him?

The train doors opened and skeletal-looking men and women in black and white striped pajamas grabbed people from the car. These inmates yelled at Nathan and the others, ordering them to step out and stand straight in a line. Nathan had to shield his eyes from the sun. He hadn't been outside for days. As they got out, the inmates hit the train passengers viciously with sticks.

Nathan felt a numbing pain in his ribs and doubled over. He had heard about these prisoners who were selected to hurt their own. It was no wonder they were totally out of their minds. The Nazis made men push their own brothers into the ovens. How could any human endure such suffering?

The group was now being separated by gender, with men shoved to the left and women to the right. Married couples were yanked viciously apart. There was much crying and shrieking as many realized they'd never see their loved ones again.

Nathan wanted to cry but fought the urge. He realized he'd probably never see Ruby again as he was led to a huge barrack.

There, SS officers surveyed the group and Nathan was put into the smaller group tasked with camp maintenance. He and five young men his age were dragged to a barber. Nathan's gold curls were chopped off roughly by a mean female SS officer with huge shears, who motioned him to sit down as she moved on to the next prisoner.

Nathan touched his raw scalp, scanning the crowd to see if he recognized anyone from the swing party. Otto was there throwing his arm around another fellow named Manny. Otto was making a good show of being cheerful despite the blood and bruises. "We're on the right side, Manny. Don't forget. We stood up to them, Manny. Remember that!"

CHAPTER THIRTY-THREE

Code Blue

I followed Mrs. B into the piano room, still processing all that she had told me. I wanted to help, but I still didn't see how.

"Let the music guide you Zoey," said Mrs B. She turned to Ruby. "You also have a great musical gift, Ruby. And you are a wonderful pilot. This journey is all about music and flight. Remember all these wonderful musicians we've lost to the skies."

We both nodded at her.

"With you, Ruby, Zoey can really soar. She will beat Zapallero at his game because she has both gifts, like you. Not many people are wonderful pilots and musicians," she said.

"I'm not a pilot, Mrs B," I protested.

Mrs. B shook her head. "You're wrong dear. You were born with wings. Can you deny the thrill you felt at first lifting off in Buddy Holly's plane?"

I recalled how wonderful I felt. It had reminded me of playing music.

"You will learn to fly Zoey, trust me," she said.

Ruby grinned. "I will be happy to give you a few flying lessons," she said.

I smiled back. In spite of our dire predicament, I felt a twinge of excitement at the prospect of learning to fly. I had never realized it before, but flying had stirred something inside of me. Mrs. B tapped a little stick on the piano to get our attention.

"For now, let's get back to the music. I think the two of you should play some more. Let's really swing," she said, humming "Moonlight Serenade" again.

"You missed Nathan by mere seconds this time," she said in a whisper. "Let the music guide you and think about Zapallero's next step. Think blues. Think jazz. Think swing. Let the music guide you. Think of the most dangerous place that Zapallero could have placed Nathan through the music."

I played and suddenly visualized that picture of the Swing Kids in the text book.

"I know where Nathan is. He's with the Swing Kids, right?" I gasped.

"Yes. You're right," said Mrs. B. "Nathan is with the Swing Kids and has gotten into terrible trouble with them. Go back to your textbook to see," she said.

But Ruby knew exactly where he was. "Nathan's in a concentration camp, right?"

Mrs. B nodded. "There are many clues in that book. Zapallero has the same book. That book holds the key." And then she kept repeating those words over and over again.

"That book holds the key. That book holds the key. That book holds the key."

Ruby and I had started improvising over "Moonlight Serenade," adding a very dissonant and eerie sound to the song, as we visualized poor Nathan in Nazi-led Germany.

But the music was soothing at the same time. We kept playing, soaring to unknown corridors in our music psyche, thinking dark thoughts about death and concentration camps.

CHAPTER THIRTY-FOUR

Back and Forth

The next time I opened my eyes, we were back in the hotel room. My eyes travelled to the poster of the Swing Kids on the wall.

I looked at Ruby and she said, "There you go." If there had been any doubt, there wasn't any now. We knew that Nathan had been morphed and was with Swing Kids.

Someone knocked again on the door. "Who is it?" asked Ruby cautiously approaching the door.

"Just us," said Tammy through the door and we opened it for her and her dad.

"We were knocking and knocking, but you guys were playing so hard you couldn't hear us," said Tammy as she came inside.

I watched her face for any trace of recognition but there was none. It didn't feel like Tammy had any sense of what we'd been through.

"We got subs. It was the closest thing we could find," said Tammy, putting down a bag of food.

Dan walked over to the window. "We managed to give them the slip, but getting past the press in the morning will be harder," he said.

"We'll figure out something. But I'm telling you now. I'm heading back to Oshkosh right after the press conference," he said, looking sharply at me. "And you are getting in that car with me, Zoey Browne."

I stared blankly at him. I wasn't in the mood to argue. What was the point? With any luck, maybe everything would be sorted out by then. We sat quietly chomping on our sandwiches. An Italian sub never tasted so good. It felt like days since I'd eaten, but then the sandwich turned to mud in my mouth as I looked again at the Swing Kids poster. The phone rang, jarring all of us.

"Who'd be calling us here?" I wondered aloud.

Dan picked up the phone. "Who is this?" he exclaimed. "I'm not giving Ruby the phone unless you identify yourself."

But Ruby stood up and gestured for Dan to give it to her. "Please give me the phone. Maybe it's someone who can help us," she said in a frantic and hushed voice.

Dan handed it to her suspiciously. "It sounds like a crank, someone with a thick German accent," he said. Ruby eagerly took the phone but by the time she put it to her ear, the line was already dead.

"Sorry," said Dan.

"It's okay. You're probably right. It was probably some crank," she said, trying to hide her disappointment. I glanced at the Swing Kids poster again, but then a big wave of fatigue overtook me. I suddenly felt so tired, I could barely think straight.

"I think we'd all better get some sleep," I said to no one in particular. Everyone agreed and Dan and Tammy stood up.

"Goodnight," said Tammy. "Don't let the bed bugs or the paparazzi bite," she said.

I hugged her. "We'll see you in the morning."

Tammy and Dan left. Ruby and I brushed our teeth and as soon as we hit our pillows, we fell fast asleep. An hour later, my cell phone rang. It was Dad.

CHAPTER THIRTY-FIVE

Textbook Case

I left the room to talk with him. I sat in the little stairwell the receptionist had shown us. Dad and I argued for an hour. He already figured I wasn't coming back so fast. And he wasn't about to let me get away with it. But I stood my ground. I told him I couldn't leave Ruby. The upshot was he was coming to Clarinda right after his show tomorrow night.

After we hung up I returned to the room and climbed back into bed. I didn't want to drag Dad into this. Zapallero had already messed with him when he was a little kid. He had been his test monkey. I would not let Tony Zapallero hurt my father again, I vowed as I lay in bed.

I had fallen back asleep for awhile but then awoke early. It was only 5 am. The press conference would be in a few hours. I felt a weird fluttering in my heart.

Was I musi-morphing again? My mind revisited the moment when I was at the controls of Buddy Holly's plane and the magnificence I had felt as the plane started to lift.

Something had changed. I had changed. I now understood the beauty and freedom of flight. No matter what happened, I'd always have that. I had gained a new attitude. It was the attitude of altitude. I had discovered that I loved flying. Mrs. B was right.

I felt giddy, high, as if I could transport myself without the music. I understood the pilot's secret but then I looked again at the poster of the Swing Kids and my mood changed. The room was dark but a streetlight shone through the window and lit up the poster as if it were under a spotlight.

I sprang out of my bed, careful not to wake up Ruby. I got my music textbook. Mrs. B had said the clues were in this textbook. I flipped the pages until I found the picture again. Below it was an explanation.

In August 1944, German police brutally arrested 300 Swing Kids in Hamburg at a party. Many were badly beaten and some were sent to concentration camps.

My mind raced as I looked at the photo, thinking of Mrs B's words.

"That book holds the key. That book holds the key. That book holds the key," Mrs. B had chanted. Just then my cell phone vibrated. I couldn't believe Dad was calling me again. But to my surprise, I saw that it was a text from Wisconsin. It was Joe. "Call me," he wrote.

Just thinking about him made me feel goofy. I really was having a crush in the middle of all this.

I didn't want to wake Ruby so I left the room again. I went outside this time. It was quiet and deserted in the parking lot at this hour. I sat behind Dan's car to stay out of sight just in case. I called Joe.

"Hey," I whispered.

"How are you?" he asked warmly.

"Okay. We're in Clarinda, Iowa," I said.

"I know. I saw the news," he said. "Have you seen the news about Cougar?"

"No."

"Zapallero's swooped up all of shares and has announced a merger with his other company, Dragonaire," he said.

"Ugh." It was disgusting how this was all just one big stupid game of Monopoly to Zapallero. With his musi-morphing powers and his growing empire, he'd ultimately control hundreds of companies, millions of people and Musicland. He'd control the world. I wanted to get him so badly.

"Zoey, I'm driving to Clarinda today," said Joe, jerking me back to earth.

First Dad and now him. This was too much. "I think you and Tammy and Ruby are in danger," he said.

"We're fine," I said, but wondered if Joe knew more than I thought. "You don't have to do that. We can take care of ourselves," I said. "We're hiding out from the press more than from anything else .We're not even sure if we're staying here."

"I'm leaving now," he said ignoring my last words. "I miss you."

My heart melted. He was so sweet. People in LA were different. Everybody was so cool there. Joe was much more open.

"Me too," I muttered.

"See you later," he said. I hung up and sat there thinking about him, wondering how I'd make it through the next few hours until I saw him again.

But as I got back to the hotel room I remembered my real purpose for being in Clarinda and it was not for the purpose of enjoying a boyfriend. I was here to save Nathan. My hearted started pounding. It sped up and slowed down. I sat, frightened. What was happening? These weren't normal heart flutters from a crush.

I was morphing into tempo. At that moment, I had the strongest urge to play something really fast on my keyboard. Ruby had managed to sleep through all my nonsense. I didn't want to disturb her now so I grabbed my backpack and walked into the small bathroom. I pulled out my keyboard and inserted my earplugs and soon my hands were flying on the keys.

And then my inner tempo slowed down and I started playing more deliberately. I had no control over these warring tempos in my body. In my mind's eye, I saw sheet music. I came upon a fermata, a little dot above a musical note that indicates a note suspended in time. It signals the musician to hold a note for a long time until the conductor cuts it.

Without realizing it I had been holding the F note down on my keyboard since the image had flashed in my mind. It had been already a minute and then another weird thing happened. The Swing Kids photo flashed in the mirror. It was everywhere.

I stopped playing to get the textbook as if I were following orders. I opened it right to the photo of the Swing Kids and put it in front of my keyboard. I felt like I was under a spell. I played slowly as I stared at the music and felt the photo drawing me in, deeper and deeper. And then I felt as if I was falling headfirst into the textbook. When I opened my eyes, I was looking at myself from inside the poster.

Had I morphed? Or had I been morphed? Could this be the handiwork of Tony Zapallero? Did he send people back using music and photography? Why hadn't anyone else thought of this? I started feeling panic. Would I ever get out of this textbook?

And then the tempo in my head shifted and I found myself back in the room playing staccato on my keyboard. I felt like a puppet.

The room shook and the familiar musi-morphing feeling shot through my veins like a warm injection. But then I felt a chill and things changed.

Suddenly I saw an image of Tony Zapallero flashing before my eyes. Another chill ripped through every bone as I found myself staring into his jackal-like grin that grew wider and wider beckoning me as the photo had done earlier. Was I being hypnotized?

And then something more ominous happened. Instead of the usual calming musical sensation I often got on these journeys, I felt a terrible stinging pain throughout my body. Everything went pitch black and grew very quiet. I felt the room lift for a few seconds but then it came back down with a thud.

The lights came back on. I could see again. I was still in the bathroom and everything seemed normal. The textbook was still in front of my keyboard, open to the picture. I felt like I'd just escaped a horrible fate after winning an arm wrestle with the devil.

CHAPTER THIRTY-SIX

Warp Speed

"Are you okay?" yelled Ruby on the other side of the door. I don't know how long she'd been standing there.

"Just a sec," I said to her, staring at myself in the mirror. Had I just imagined all that? His sinister smile had seemed so real and the pain had been torture.

But I checked myself and nothing seemed different. I had just barely escaped being "zapped" to another universe by Tony Zapallero, I realized. Now I was certain that something had happened to Joe and I when we had gone to the practice room at Cougar.

Again I thought of Mrs B's words: "That book holds the key. That book holds the key. That book holds the key."

I opened the door. Ruby stared at me suspiciously.

"Something really strange just happened. I have to call Joe," I said, walking past her towards my bed.

Joe sounded surprised to hear from me.

"Sorry to do this but I have to ask a favor of you." I sounded so bossy I wanted to die. But I had no choice. This was important.

"What do you need?" he asked.

"I need you to go back to Cougar."

Dead silence on the other end. "Why?" Joe asked curtly. I regretted it immediately. What had I been thinking?

"Sorry. Never mind. It was just a hunch I had." I knew I was blowing this relationship and investigation big time. But then Joe Leonard surprised me like he always does.

"What are you looking for?" he asked. Joe Leonard really was the coolest guy I had ever met in a sweet Midwestern sort of way.

"I know this sounds crazy, but I'm looking for a textbook," I said holding my breath and praying Joe didn't get totally disgusted with me.

"Can you be a little more specific?" He did not sound excited. But I'd soon find out that Joe had some reasons of his own for looking around Zapallero's office.

"I know it seems nutty but I really can't explain it right now. Let's just say I think it will give us some clues into what he's thinking," I stammered.

There was another long pause. 'It's easy enough. I have the card key. I can just walk right in there. It used to be my dad's office and Zapallero never changed the security code."

"That's awesome. Be careful," I said, hating the fact that I'd have to wait longer to see Joe. What was the use anyway? I'd be back in LA in the fall and he'd be back in college. He seemed like he actually liked me. And now I had just delayed seeing him for many more hours. I felt depressed when I got off the phone.

"Are you okay?" asked Ruby, now holding the textbook.

"No," I said. I felt like crying. "He was all set to come here. But now Joe's going to poke around Zapallero's office for the textbook," I said despondently.

Ruby sat next to me pointing at the Swing Kids picture in the textbook. "What happened to you?" she asked.

"Zapallero almost sent me there," I said referring to the Swing Kids. "I felt myself being morphed but I managed to stop him."

Ruby hugged me. "These kids got into big trouble. I'm glad you stopped him," she said with worry in her voice.

I nodded. "Some of the Swing Kids even died in the camps," I said, looking into her eyes. She looked away as tears filled her eyes.

"So Zapallero grabs a sample of someone's musical DNA and embeds it in a device that somehow programs that person to play a song, which at some point hits a pause. Somehow he suspends that pause in the music. And by doing so, he's stopping the music, which in a way is like stopping time." It almost sounded like it made sense as the words rolled off my tongue.

I think I got it now. Zapallero had somehow untangled the complex metabolic structure of music and figured out had to wedge a portal through it. I had learned that all music exists in a moving state of time. It is fluid and bounces back and forth from the earth like an ocean wave fuelled by gravity and rhythm.

"He stops time?" Ruby repeated.

"We all do when we morph. But Zap can predetermine a person's journey with the technology he has developed," I said.

"And Mrs. B said the book held the clues," said Ruby nodding. "You think we can figure out Zapallero's next move if we get the book?"

"I hope so. He's probably got a whole musi-morphing road map in there," I said.

Ruby looked at her watch. The news conference was in less than an hour.

CHAPTER THIRTY-SEVEN

Camp Clarinda

We got to the press conference in time to hear officials talking about the bizarre discovery. The Clarinda mayor stood in front of the Glenn Miller Museum and showed a Power Point slide of Nathan's wallet in a Ziploc bag.

The mayor loved his fifteen minutes of fame. Clarinda didn't get on the national news very often. Everyone from CNN to ABC and CBS was there in full force.

"Ladies and gentlemen." Clarinda Mayor John Kane looked boyish despite his silver hair. The mayor was flanked on either side by police officials.

"I know we're all baffled by this case and so I'll cut right to the chase. Just minutes ago, another item of Nathan Gordon's was found right here in Clarinda," he said. The crowd stirred. This was news. Reporters stirred impatiently.

"I just got a call from a security guard at Camp Clarinda across town. He said they found keys there. It turns out those keys belong to Nathan Gordon!"

Some reporters began packing up. Everyone wanted to go to Camp Clarinda, whatever that was.

"What's Camp Clarinda?" asked Ruby raising her hand. Other reporters chimed in, less politely, barking questions at Mayor Kane.

"Where is Camp Clarinda? When were the keys found? Did they suspect foul play?" A police officer took the mike from the mayor, who was quickly getting flustered.

"We're working with the FBI and have no further comments about the Nathan Gordon investigation at this time. But I can tell you a little about Camp Clarinda..." he said. Most of the reporters left mid-sentence. They could always Google Camp Clarinda. They had deadlines to meet.

But Ruby and I stayed as the policeman rattled on. "Camp Clarinda was a POW camp during World War II." We both looked at each other. We were sure that Nathan had morphed back to a concentration camp. But could he now be in this POW camp? That would still place him in the 1940s.

We were getting a big history lesson about World War II. The policeman explained that by the end of the war, hundreds of thousands of European and Japanese soldiers were imprisoned in America. Many were sent to camps in Iowa to help harvest crops, build roads and move trees.

Many of these men returned to Europe after the war but were changed by the experience. They had seen an

America that was different than the propaganda they'd been fed. Some had liked it here in fact. But others hated America more than ever. For some Germans, their time in the prison only served to further fuel their Nazi loyalties, which made for tense moments in camps like Clarinda.

"We need to get over to that museum as fast as possible," I said to Tammy, Ruby and Dan as the policeman wrapped up his tutorial.

Had Nathan morphed there? If so, it was better than a concentration camp.

Mayor Kane got back on the mike and urged everyone to try some of Clarinda's fine restaurants.

I heard some reporters talking. National interest in the story was picking up. Had Nathan disappeared because of a terrorist plot? Or was an alien invasion to blame? People were getting scared. Kidnappings, abductions, unsolved mysteries happen all the time. But this wasn't like anything anyone had seen before, particularly with all these bizarre clues that kept popping up.

We got in the car and Dan drove us to Camp Clarinda. It wasn't far from the Glenn Miller Museum.

"This is it. I'm done," said Dan as we pulled up to camp, which was now a museum. "I'm heading back to Oshkosh with Tammy. I spoke with your dad, Zoey. You are to wait for him at the hotel. Do you understand?"

I nodded. I hated to say goodbye to Tammy and Dan but was relieved at the same time. I didn't want to get them mixed up in any more of this. I had a feeling we were closing in on Nathan's path and things might get ugly.

I hugged Tammy. "I'll see you in LA," I said. She hugged back and now I had a feeling she knew exactly what was going on, but wasn't saying. I looked into her eyes but she looked away.

"Be careful," she said. She and her dad got in their car and Dan started the engine.

I watched the car drive off, missing her immediately. Ruby and I stood in front of the Camp Clarinda for a few minutes to collect our thoughts.

I looked around to see if I could detect anything that may lead me to Nathan.

Camp Clarinda consisted of a little museum that housed artifacts and pictures and a small bunker that had been restored to look like a room where prisoners slept during the war. One of the museum workers was showing reporters around.

We tagged along on the tour and walked into the bunker. Inside were bunk beds, lockers, cubbies with personal effects like toothbrushes. A camp mailbox and military office equipment were also on display, along with some framed letters from a prisoner and photos of camp life.

In this bunker was a painting by a German prisoner named Franz Bauer. Below his painting, a plaque said that Bauer had stayed at the camp from 1943 to 1945 but had returned to the United States after the war. I guess Franz had been one of the prisoners who liked America.

"We found Nathan's keys near Bauer's paintings," said the museum worker. "Forensic investigators are searching for more clues, but have found nothing other than Nathan's prints on the keys."

"Does Nathan have any relatives in Clarinda?" asked one reporter.

"Not that we know of," said the guide.

My phone vibrated. It was Joe. "Be right back," I said to Ruby as I hurried outside.

CHAPTER THIRTY-EIGHT

Office Politics

"Hey," said Joe. "I'm in." Joe had just walked right in without a problem. He was, after all, the son of the founder.

Few people ever went up to the penthouse level and Joe knew Zapallero wasn't around. He'd heard from some friends at the airport that Zapallero had left Wisconsin in a private jet the night before.

"I hope I haven't sent you on a wild goose chase," I said into the phone.

"Oh, c'mon I haven't had this much fun in a long time," said Joe playfully.

"Very funny," I said.

"I'm not kidding. I like hanging out with girls who play keyboard in hangars in the middle of the night," he said.

I didn't know what to say. Was he flirting? I still couldn't believe my luck. Why would someone like Joe Leonard be interested in me?

I suspected it was because we both hated Zapallero so much. Joe wanted to get him as badly as I did. Yes we did have that in common.

And then I thought of my otherworldly experience in the motel earlier that morning. Zapallero must have been messing with our DNA since we had walked into the practice room on the night that Nathan had disappeared. He'd been zapping me around Musicland ever since. I worried about Joe. I wondered if he had experienced anything similar.

"Have you noticed any more music-related clues?" I said dancing around the topic.

There was a pause. "Not exactly. But I've gotten back into the drums in the last few days. I'm not sure why but it feels good," he said.

Joe had told me over our pancake breakfast that he briefly played drums and had enjoyed it. But he said he had dropped the instrument when his father died. His dad had been his biggest fan. Joe's dad didn't have a musical bone in his body and thought anyone who did was magical.

"Forget Cougar, forget flying. Forget engineering. If I could make music the way you make music, I'd do that," his father had told him.

But Joe said his mother had strongly disagreed, noting that most musicians barely earned a living.

Joe told me he had given it up and had never looked back. He didn't think he was any good. Nobody but his father had ever been that impressed.

But then in the last 24 hours, he had been haunted by a constant drumbeat in his head. It was maddening. He had dug up his drumsticks and started fooling around on his old set in his mother's garage. And it had felt great.

Hearing him describe this confirmed my suspicions. Something must have definitely happened to Joe and I in the practice room at Cougar the night we snooped around. Zapallero had begun brainwashing us.

But I didn't have time to go into that with Joe right now. He was already on his way up to Zapallero's suite. Joe told me he had walked right into the building early in the morning.

"Hey Joe! Long time no see," said a guard sitting at the reception desk and watching TV.

"Hey Marty. I'm in town for the air show and I came by for a few things," Joe said, trying to sound nonchalant.

"Cool. Go right up. How's school?" said the guard cheerfully.

"Good, thanks," said Joe with a big smile as he walked swiftly to the elevator. He rode up to the third floor, which was filled with cubicles.

He'd been working on this floor during school holidays and went over to his desk to make it look authentic, he said. Joe pulled out some old receipts and looked around, but didn't see anyone so he slipped into the nearest stairwell and jogged up two steps at a time to the top floor and to Zapallero's suite.

It was fancier up here, with marble walls and floors. Joe waved a card near a door that opened into Zapellero's office. He stepped in and a rush of memories came to him. He'd spent a lot of time up here. His mom would sometimes work long hours, so his dad would get him from school and bring him here.

But Joe said the room was different now. The biggest change was a gigantic portrait of Zapallero with the president of the United States directly above his desk.

Hearing about the photo gave me a start. I hadn't realized how many powerful people Zapallero knew.

He said the room also had been refurnished with modern furniture. One wall was lined floor to ceiling with bookshelves.

"Wow," said Joe. "There's that beat in my head again that I just can't shake."

"I think Zapallero did something to us when we went to the practice room the other night," I said. "I've been hearing a beat in my head too."

"What?" said Joe.

"I know it sounds crazy. But I think he's patented some technology that interacts with people's.... musicality," I tried to explain.

"Are you kidding me?" said Joe

CHAPTER THIRTY-NINE

Bookwormhole

"I'm dead serious. That's why I need you to find that book," I said.

"Ok. Well I'm here in the office and I'm looking at thousands of books," Joe said.

"Is there a system to the way the books are sorted? Is there a music section?" I whispered as more journalists began arriving at Camp Clarinda.

"There are so many," said Joe, stepping closer to the bookshelves to scan titles. "There are business books, history books and aviation books. Hmm, there's a whole section of hypnosis books."

There was a brief pause.

"Here are some music books!" Joe exclaimed.

"Cool. Do you see anything that says the *Fundamentals of Music*?"

"Lots of biographies, history books and volumes on Jazz and other genres," he ticked off. "Hmm. There are a lot of scientific books on the brain and music," he said.

"You may want to grab one of those," I said. "But I'm looking specifically for that textbook."

"I see it!" he exclaimed excitedly.

"Grab it!" I said, praying this would help us figure out where Zapallero was going next. I hoped Joe wasn't in danger. I had a terrible feeling that Zap may have laid another trap for us. "You should get out of there!" I whispered.

"Okay. I just want to find something....ouch!" he yelped all of a sudden.

"I just got a bad pain in my chest. It's like the beat in my head is now speeding up my heart or something," he said. "It's really intense. I have to sit down."

"Joe! Joe!" I practically screamed into the phone. I was worried sick. "Please get out of there. He's doing this to you. I think you're in danger."

I hated myself for sending him there. What had I been thinking?

There was just silence on the other end. I held my breath for a few seconds. I thought of calling 911, but then I heard something that indicated life. It was the sound of drumming.

Joe had actually picked up two pencils on Zapallero's desk and had started tapping out the rhythm section to "Moonlight Serenade".

"Is that you drumming Joe? Please talk to me," I urged him.

"I...can't...stop ....myself...from....playing," Joe said with great effort on the other end. "The picture...."

I got a terrible knot in my stomach. Was Zapallero morphing Joe right then and there?

The answer was yes. Joe at that very moment was staring into the textbook, which had fallen to the floor and lay open to the picture of the Swing Kids.

The picture was drawing him in. "Don't look at it!" I exclaimed.

I heard nothing except for the eerie persistent tap of his drumming.

If I'd been there with Joe, I would see he was experiencing what I had just gone through in the motel bathroom. Joe was being pulled against his will into the picture. Within seconds it was as if he was totally sucked into it. He felt like he was now on the inside of the textbook, looking out into a ghastly image of Zapallero's leering face.

Joe, are you all right? Can you hear me?"

I heard nothing for what felt like an eternity. And then I heard a huge thud. It was actually the sound of the book being hurled across the room by Joe.

And then I heard his voice and I felt like screaming with joy.

"Zoey, I'm fine," he said. "I'm okay but something really crazy just happened," he said.

"You've got to get out of there, please," I begged him.

"I will. I just want to look through some of his papers," said Joe who was now rummaging through Zapallero's desk drawer.

Joe stopped as he came across some financial documents.

"This guy had his hands in everything," he said. "You should see this. He owns big stakes in gaming companies, oil companies, toy companies and even clothing companies. He must be worth billions," he said whistling.

I was sure this was all good information but I didn't think it was worth risking his safety over. "Eureka!" he exclaimed. "I found what I've been looking for. Here are the stock certificates in my father's name. A lot of them," he said triumphantly.

"He's going to have to buy me out to get control of this company," he added, scooping up the certificates. I was happy he found what he'd been looking for.

"Get out of there please!" I persisted.

"Ok," said Joe, stuffing the book and the certificates in his backpack. Joe was just about to leave when he heard footsteps in the hallway outside.

"Gotta go!" he exclaimed. The phone went dead.

I couldn't stand this anymore. I wondered if I'd ever see Joe again. What happened if he got hurt or got in trouble? Could he be arrested for trespassing? It was my entire fault.

I felt as if my head was going to explode.

Joe had snuck into the little space under Zapallero's desk when the door swung open and a cleaning woman named Rosa entered. Joe held his breath.

Rosa came dangerously close to the desk to dust but after a few minutes, she moved on to the big easy chair in the corner. Luckily, she wasn't the deepest of cleaners. She dusted the bookshelf next. Joe let out a little sigh of relief. He seemed to be heading for the homestretch now.

But then Rosa's phone rang. She sat down to answer.

"Hi. Oh yes. That was a few days ago. The pilot disappeared. I know. Mr. Zapallero gave me $500 to bring sheet of music over the air show on that same day. Yes, I'm serious," she said laughing. "I just gave it to John Kiefer by the hangar. He said he'd give me more jobs like that. What do you mean I'll get in trouble?" her tone had turned defensive.

"How could sheet music be illegal? What are you loco?"

Rosa ended the call, absently ran a vacuum over a tiny piece of the carpet and left the room. Joe waited for a few minutes before he crawled out from under the desk. He was panting and his legs were shaking.

He looked up at the picture of Zapallero with the president and felt a knot in his stomach. He had the feeling he was in something far bigger than he'd originally thought.

Just as he was about to slip out of the door, something else caught his eye. On a small table by one of the arm chairs was a basket holding several small iPods.

On a whim, Joe scooped them up and threw them in his backpack. Then he ran out the door, slipping down the stairwell and running down three at a time until he reached the main lobby.

He'd been in the building all of thirty minutes, but it had felt like an eternity. He walked by the security guard, trying to appear calm.

"Thanks a lot, Marty," he said giving him a wink but not breaking his stride.

"Take it easy Joe. Stop by again soon," said the guard barely taking his eyes off the TV. Once safely in his car, he called me again.

"I was so worried! I'm sorry," I said, sobbing.

"It's okay. It was just a cleaning woman, but I had to hide until she left," he said. "I'm heading to Clarinda. See you in a few hours," he said, adding quietly, "Don't worry. I'm okay."

"Okay," I said, smiling into the phone. "Thank you. See you soon."

CHAPTER FORTY

Trading Places

Nathan told me he would never forget his time in the camps. After one day in the first concentration camp, he was transported to another, which seemed better at first. There were cement buildings instead of wooden barracks and little gardens scattered about. He got to take a hot shower there.

But afterwards, he was ordered to wait outside, shivering for an hour in the freezing cold. Then he was told to run to another barrack. There, a new guard with kind eyes greeted him.

"You're in a place of death and suffering. But you have the strength to survive and you will if you believe that," he said. The next few days passed rather uneventfully but Nathan kept thinking about the guard's words, which gave him hope.

There was little to do but wait from each tiny meal to the next. Nathan grew thinner and thinner. He thought of home and missed Ruby. One night as he got ready for bed the nice guard came over to him.

"I'm getting removed. They think I'm too nice. They will probably kill me," the guard said matter-of-factly. Nathan looked at him, shocked.

"You have the strength to survive and you will if you believe that," Nathan said, repeating the words the guard had said to him days earlier. The guard smiled at him and they didn't see each other for days. Nathan thought he'd never see him again.

During those long days, Nathan tried to summon up that musical feeling that seemed to send him across space and time. But it didn't work. He tried it again at night when he and the other prisoners lay on their cots, trying to sing. Nathan barely had the energy to hum, but he persisted.

One night as he lay in his cot humming, the kind guard returned and stared at him from the entrance of the barrack. Who was he? Nathan thought he looked familiar.

The guard beckoned to Nathan, who got up, again surprised by this guard's curious actions. But when he saw him close up, he realized he knew the older man.

The guard was actually John Kiefer. Nathan had not recognized him because he was so much thinner now and wore a scraggly beard. The last time he had seen Kiefer was when the older man had insisted on flying Glenn Miller's plane instead of him.

Kiefer told him that he had barely stepped into Miller's plane when Zapallero had morphed him again. Zapallero had big plans for Kiefer. He wanted him back at Cougar.

But Kiefer had outsmarted him this time. After all his morphing in the past few days, Kiefer's powers had strengthened considerably. He was determined to save Nathan and had managed to direct himself to the concentration camp where Nathan had gone.

"Can you help me get home?" Nathan whispered hopefully as they stood near the barrack entrance. Kiefer shook his head. "I can get you out of here but you still have to find your own musical path back home. You just have to let the music guide you, once I get you off Zapallero's radar."

Nathan had so many questions but Kiefer shook his head. "It's not safe to talk here. Let's go outside."

They walked to a dark space in between two barracks. Kiefer motioned for Nathan to quickly get undressed.

"Let's swap clothes. You'll be safer in my uniform," said Kiefer. Nathan tried to protest at first, but then complied.

"I'm not giving you a ticket to paradise," Kiefer said as he put on Nathan's striped pajamas. "The other guards are out to get me, so you have to leave tonight. But you'll have better luck in an SS uniform than in these," he said, buttoning up the prisoner's shirt.

And just like that, Nathan slipped into the night in a German uniform. He didn't get very far. Within hours, he was captured by Allied soldiers and was taken as a prisoner and transported to a POW camp in the U.S. And that's how Nathan's keys were found in Camp Clarinda.

CHAPTER FORTY-ONE

Music Nazis

I sat on the steps in front of Camp Clarinda with Ruby and closed my eyes. "I'm going to take a walk to clear my head a little," said Ruby.

"Be careful," I said, appreciating a little alone time. It had been an exhausting day. I needed a moment to get my thoughts together before Joe arrived.

But then the beating returned.

I tried to shove it from my mind as I pulled the textbook from my backpack again. The book seemed to have a life of its own. When I opened it, the pages flipped right to the picture of the Ghetto Swingers this time.

I knew I should try to shut the book, but I couldn't resist looking at the photo of the Jewish prisoners who had been ordered to play swing for a propaganda film before they were coldly executed. It filled me with sadness, looking at the musicians with big yellow Jewish stars emblazoned on their jackets.

I couldn't comprehend how human beings could inflict such pain on one another. It was scary how an entire nation had fallen in line behind one evil man with a terrible vision.

After staring at the doomed band members in the picture, my eyes wandered to a row of Nazi guards standing against a wall behind them. Their faces were totally impassive. Could every one of those guards have been true believers? Or were they just afraid to defy Hitler?

I had learned about resistance by the Swing Kids, but knew that most Germans were afraid to defy Hitler.

I wondered what it had been like here in Clarinda during those years, as I stared at the guards in the photo. Had any of those soldiers wound up here as prisoners in Camp Clarinda?

Maybe some had and were actually happy to get out of Germany after being drafted into the Nazi Youth as kids. Plucking corn in Iowa and listening to swing music might have been a nice change.

My heart started to accelerate again as the image of those Nazi soldiers in the photo burned in my brain. I felt the picture drawing me in, like the Swing Kids photo had done earlier that day. And then there was that sensation of diving head first into the textbook.

Within minutes, I felt like I was inside the picture. And again, I had the feeling that Zapallero was controlling me like a puppet on a string.

The familiar musi-morphing feeling started to wash through me and I started feeling the ground beneath me shake. I fought the iciness that coursed through my veins.

And soon I no longer felt like I was inside the picture. I was back to sitting on the steps. Music blared in my head. It was so loud I couldn't think straight. But I willed myself to pull out my keyboard and started playing something, anything to drown out the song that was now beating in my head. It worked!

The beating stopped and I sank back against the building, exhausted. Again I felt like I had just been in a battle with evil and had won. I was getting closer to Zapallero, I could feel it. And I felt my own powers getting stronger with each confrontation.

CHAPTER FORTY-TWO

Evil Plotter

Tony Zapallero was in fact dangerously close. He was just a few blocks away at that very moment. He stared through the window of his hotel room in the Clarinda Marriott, watching the hot afternoon sun gleam over the countryside and thought about how he was going to destroy me.

He had just tried to zap me back into World War II but had failed. Zapallero was finding me to be more and more of nuisance. He couldn't believe I was holding my own against his powers. But it was only a matter of time. He had big plans.

He was one of the richest men in the country, but he wanted more. Cougar had shown him what was possible. Even though it wasn't his biggest acquisition, Cougar was his most important to date. It had shown him what he could do when he applied his theory about musical DNA to technology.

He had managed to rig up the practice room at the Cougar headquarters and had morphed Nathan and that pesky Kiefer across time and space. Those iPod players were the key, he thought, chuckling. He had programmed them with all the music of the artists who died in flight.

It had all worked beautifully until Kiefer started acting up. And then the girl kept messing him up too. He scowled as he thought about me. Some people were stronger than he thought

Maybe he'd been overzealous by making Nathan disappear in front of so many people. But it didn't matter. Once he moved around a few more people, he'd have so much money and power, nobody could mess with him. He'd have castles in Europe and ranches in Africa and islands in the Pacific.

The world would be just one gigantic playground for Tony Zapallero. Of course there'd be no music. He'd have to control the music and pause it. But who cared? It would all be his.

His technology was so strong because it was fueled by the artistic spirit of humans. Tony Zapallero hadn't been able to enter Musicland for years but with the DNA of that little prodigy Paul from Indiana, he had rigged an intensely powerful device that could morph humans across time for centuries to come.

He'd spent years perfecting his theory, all the while keeping his idea quiet. His employees had no idea what was going on beyond the fact that they were trying to build a computer that ran on the power of melody. But when they left at night, Zapallero would go into the lab and play his keyboard, staring into the computer screen and feel himself being absorbed right into the image.

With some adjusting, he could send anyone back to any image he placed on the screen. As computer technology advanced, and more memory could be loaded onto tinier chips, he managed to transfer these functions to smaller and smaller devices. Eventually all he needed was a tiny iPod to send people to the musical universe.

All Zap needed to do was push a button and he could direct people anywhere, if he had a sample of their musical DNA.

Or so he thought. Something about that girl was tripping him up. I knew what it was. I had my dad's DNA, that's what.

But Zapallero didn't know that as he looked at a newspaper sitting on a desk in his hotel room. The front page was covered with the story of how Nathan's keys had been found at the POW camp in Clarinda, Iowa.

He had not planned for that to happen either. How had Nathan wound up there? He was supposed to die in the concentration camp, Zapallero thought as he looked at the newspaper.

Had Kiefer gotten his hands on one of his iPods? That joker kept morphing himself to wherever Zapallero was sending Nathan, Zap thought, swearing under his breath. It didn't matter, he told himself. He'd show them all. He had rigged up some devices with several samples of young Paul's DNA. It was so strong that no single human being could possibly thwart it; he thought with a mad gleam in his eyes and pushed the button.

CHAPTER FORTY-THREE

Camp

I was back in the motel when he pushed the button. Exhausted from my earlier confrontation with Zapallero, I had convinced Ruby to go back to the room to rest for a while. We took a cab there. I got into bed with the music textbook. I was determined to figure out Zap's next move, but soon fell asleep.

A little while later, I was jarred awake by that terrible and painful beating in my head. The beating was sharper and more intense than ever. I felt light-headed and panicky as the rapid tempo took my body captive.

My body began to shake uncontrollably and then a blinding light blocked out everything around me. I saw Tony Zapallero's awful face looming over me, expanding into the size of a blown-up Thanksgiving Day float with his greased back jet-black hair melting into a pitch-black midnight sky.

I began to sink into a black hole for a few moments before flickering lights flashed in front of my eyes, setting up a musical staff and notes in front me as far as my eyes could see. I felt like I was in a darkened theater watching a

3D movie. But then I was in the movie, floating through the notations on this otherworldly piece of sheet music.

I felt like the bouncing ball, driving atop the musical notes towards a pulsating pause sign that stretched slightly this way and that. Then the pause sign changed shape, expanding one second, contracting the next before yawning into a gigantic black hole that pulled me in. As I felt myself being sucked into the pause sign, I heard a loud, piercing shriek, followed by utter darkness and silence. I'd later compare notes with Nathan and see that this was virtually identical to his experience when he'd been zapped.

As I moved through the darkness and silence, I saw a purple light glowing in the distance. Another shock rippled through my body and I landed on my feet, darts of pain shooting up my legs. I winced from the pain, blinking and shielding my eyes against intense sunlight. A shrieking sound filled the air again. And then there was the sound of birds chirping. The air felt cold. I was standing among a crowd of people.

My hands were clenched so tight, it hurt to open them. When I did, something fell to the ground. Startled, I bent to pick it up. It was my hotel room key card with a picture of the Glenn Miller Inn on it. I had been using it as a bookmark. I must have fallen asleep with it in my hand before I morphed.

Someone pushed me roughly from behind as I noticed a horrible stench in the air. I'd soon learn it was the putrid odor of burning flesh. To the right and left of me were young and old people. Everyone looked terribly sad.

Mean-looking emaciated people in striped uniforms were ushering us towards a concrete barracks. They wielded flashlights and sticks.

"Hurry, hurry!" they said in dead voices. They randomly hit people in the line with their sticks. I felt like I was in a teen zombie movie, although nobody here was wearing makeup or pretending.

I was in a concentration camp. Zapallero had sent me here. He had finally done it. I might not make it out of here alive, I realized as I walked with the other unfortunate souls. A tall chimney coughed out flames and black smoke into the bright blue sky. It was a picture perfect day.

"We have to get out of here Zoey, for God's sake we have to get out of here," someone said. I looked around and was shocked to see Joe.

"How did you get here?" I stammered.

"The same way you did. He programmed us the night we went to Cougar." Despite our predicament, I was shocked by how much Joe knew and understood. And I had to admit, I was happy to have him there.

But then Nazi officers came and separated the men from the women and Joe was yanked roughly from my side. Our eyes met briefly as he was herded away. Would I ever see him again? Would I ever see my mother and my father?

Was there a way out of here? And even if I did get away, how would I ever forget that smell? Would I ever get it out of my nostrils?

Out of the corner of my eye, I saw a guard throw himself on a young man, beating him in the head like a wild beast. Blood spurted from the young man who grew limp as the guard crushed him with his blows. Afterwards, he lay crumpled and dead. And then I saw the worst thing of all as the soldier ordered the prisoners to walk over the poor boy's body.

Some prisoners objected but then quieted down when the soldier raised his stick. The group fell into an obedient silence, stomping over the body again and again.

I stared at the boy's unrecognizable body for a minute and then the SS guards called on some inmates to clean up the "mess." Two men came over and started moving the body. They both had haunted looks on their faces, but one of them looked familiar. When he looked up I recognized him. It was John Kiefer.

CHAPTER FORTY-FOUR

Music Mayhem

I witnessed unimaginable acts. I'd read about the Holocaust but no one could really imagine what it was like to live it. I spotted Joe around the camp, looking forlorn. I blamed myself for getting him involved. I looked for Kiefer again, but didn't see him.

On our third day there, the guards gathered men and women together by tall black gallows. They wanted us to watch prisoners being hung for some act of disobedience.

The soldiers marched three young inmates, one boy who was only eleven, out on the platform. I couldn't take my eyes off of the boy when all of a sudden a bony finger jabbed me from behind. I looked around and saw Kiefer standing there. My heart filled with hope.

"Are you all right?" he asked.

"Yes," It was true. I'd lost weight and slept little but nobody had laid a finger on me.

"That's good. Joe is fine as well," he said looking ahead and keeping his voice as even as possible. "Do you still have that picture?" He had moved up a little so that now he was standing next to me. It was easier to speak.

"Do you mean the key card with the hotel on it?" I asked.

"Yes. Joe saw you picking it up on the first day. That picture is our ticket. You still have it, right?"

I nodded. I had put it in my shoe. Kiefer pulled aside his pajama top revealing what looked like an iPod. I gawked. It was strange to see the elegant device in the middle of a World War II concentration camp.

"Come to the watch tower at midnight," he said and then disappeared into the crowd. I scanned the crowd but didn't see him again. I felt the key card beneath my foot. Were that photo and tiny device really going to get us out of here? I prayed they would.

CHAPTER FORTY-FIVE

There's No Place Like Iowa

A few hours later, I stood with Kiefer and Joe at the watchtower. It had been surprisingly easy to sneak away from the bunker at night. Everyone had been asleep and there was no guard on duty.

When I got to the watchtower, I hugged Joe for a long time. He felt bonier than he had during our hug in the car just a few days ago.

Kiefer pulled out his iPod.

"That's it?" I asked incredulously. "That's how Zapallero moves us from place to place?"

Kiefer looked around nervously. Satisfied nobody was watching, he started to explain the principle upon which this "synthesized" musi-morphing occurred.

"Have you ever thought about the connection between musical sound and the human body?" he asked.

"Sure. Music makes you feel happy or sad," said Joe.

"Or it makes you want to dance," I added. Joe smiled at me.

"That's right," said Kiefer. "But that's just the tip of the iceberg. There's a whole new science based on how music is actually encoded in our bodies and brains. It triggers emotions and movements in a way that nothing else does. Scientists are now studying how music has affected the evolution of our species," he said.

So far this made sense, I thought.

Kiefer went on, "Zapallero worked with a lot of scientists for a long time. He realized early on that the pulse in music impacts people so strongly because everyone has certain so-called built-in clocks."

"Built-in clocks?" I repeated.

"Yes. Like a person's heartbeat or respiratory rate or even blood pressure. All these things have rhythmic systems that make people unique, like fingerprints. And the rhythms of music correspond to these organic rhythms in people," he said.

I nodded.

"So Zapallero figured out a way to stop both and actually cut a sliver through time," he said. "He figured if music is in fact encoded in our brains and our bodies, he can rewrite that code."

We heard shouting from somewhere across the camp. "We'd better move fast if we want to get out of here alive," said Joe.

Kiefer nodded. "Do you have the photo?" he asked me. I had tucked it into the waistband of my pants. I handed it to Kiefer but he handed it back to me and motioned for Joe and me to hold the card together.

"Do you know a Glenn Miller song?" he asked.

"Are you serious?" I asked, feeling ridiculous.

"Dead serious," said Kiefer. I looked at Joe and he smiled sadly at me, shrugging. I guess we might as well try anything at this point.

I started humming "Moonlight Serenade" and stared hard at the picture. Out of the corner of my eye I saw Kiefer pressing a button on his iPod.

CHAPTER FORTY-SIX

Good versus Evil

A nd then I was back in my hotel room in Clarinda. Ruby was still asleep on the bed next to me. It was as if I had never been in the concentration camp. Someone knocked on the door. Ruby stirred.

"Who is it?" I asked, cautiously getting up from my bed.

"It's me." I recognized that voice and eagerly opened the door. Joe stood smiling at me. He looked perfect, better than perfect.

"You okay?" he whispered. I nodded and we hugged a long time. He didn't feel bony anymore.

"Did that really just happen?" I asked. Joe nodded.

"I have something to show you," he said, his eyes shining. And then he opened his backpack to reveal a pile of iPods. "Guess where I got these!" he exclaimed.

"Zapallero?" I gasped.

"Yes. They were sitting right there in his office."

I LOVED this guy I thought and suddenly knew exactly what we had to do. Kiefer had told us he'd switch places with Nathan in the camp. And then he heard that Nathan had been captured by Allied forces.

"We've got to get over to Camp Clarinda," I said. Ruby was now wide awake and staring at both of us.

"You wouldn't believe where we've been," I started to explain.

CHAPTER FORTY-SEVEN

Plan Z

We walked to Joe's car and drove to Camp Clarinda. I tried to talk Ruby out of coming with us, but she insisted.

We went to the bunker. Something creeped me out. I couldn't put my finger on it until I turned around and found myself staring into the beady eyes of Tony Zapallero.

I broke into a sweat. He must've been shocked as well to see me there alive and well. I cleared my throat. "We met at the air show in Oshkosh," I said.

He smirked, looking around to see if anyone else was listening. A few reporters were milling around.

"Yes. That's correct. And I think we've been ahem, 'travelling' in some of the same circles since then too," he said with a sneer and then looked at his watch. "Think we'd better get over to the lawn for the next presser, shall we?"

As he turned to leave, he looked one last time around the bunker. "Poor guys. Doesn't look like the best accommodations, does it? Although some of these POWs actually liked it here," he said sinisterly.

"I know one in particular who really enjoyed the American music, but some of his fellow POWs didn't like that," he said. And then he turned around and left.

Joe walked over to us. "Hey. What happened? You look like you've seen a ghost."

"We just saw Zapallero and it was very strange. He was saying some strange things about a prisoner here," I said.

I felt Nathan there. It was the strangest sensation. I had the distinct feeling he was there but in another time. I looked around for some clue that would confirm my suspicions.

My musiator skills seemed finely-tuned, as if my musi-morphing abilities had strengthened in the past few days with all this activity.

And then the source of those powers, the origin of my musical DNA, walked right in the room.

"Zoey!"

I turned around stunned and let out a mice-like squeak. My dad, rock idol David Peer, was approaching me.

"Dad! I thought you were coming here after the show tonight," I exclaimed as he threw his arms around me.

He pulled away to study my face. "I cancelled the show. I had a bad feeling about all of this, a bad feeling about you," he said, looking intently into my eyes.

I still didn't know how to process this whole father-daughter thing. Here was a man, who didn't even know I existed three years ago, telling me he worried about me. I'd never known a father's love before. I had been okay on my own with my mom. And there were other new feelings I'd never felt before.

I wanted to protect him. I wanted to keep him safe from this monster that had treated him like an animal when he was just a poor little kid named Paul Osborne.

"Cougar's being bought by Tony Zapallero," I said.

Dad nodded. "I know about Tony Zapallero," he said.

"You remember him?" The image of my father wired up like a specimen made me want to hurt Zapallero.

"I do," said Dad. "I know he made Nathan vanish."

Right then I knew that he knew. We could break the code of silence. At least Zapallero had given us something. He was our clue. Dad and I had finally connected on something that linked us back to Musicland. We both knew we had morphed and we could speak about it. There was only one way Zapallero could make Nathan vanish and by knowing that, my father had acknowledged his musiator status.

Joe and Ruby had been staring at us curiously. Dad and I would have to talk later.

"Um. Dad this is Joe," I said with a tiny smile. They shook hands. I felt awkward, wondering if this was how it felt to be a normal girl introducing a normal dad to a normal guy. But I could never know what that average girl felt like, I reminded myself. No way. My Dad was meeting Joe in the middle of an epic battle between good and evil.

"Nice meeting you," said Joe. "Zoey never told me who you were, but I figured it out for myself," he said, smiling mischievously.

I looked at him, surprised, but then realized that nothing should surprise me anymore. Joe Leonard wasn't the simple farm boy I had thought. He had an edge. He was deep. Joe had soul. All these things made me even crazier about him. But I had to stop. This wasn't some romantic getaway. We needed to act soon and act fast.

"I'm Ruby."

"Sorry Ruby," I said, feeling like such a mess with all these conflicting emotions. "Dad, this is Ruby. You must have seen her on TV, right?"

"Yes. I recognize you from the news," said Dad.

I took Dad's hand and started walking towards the door. "Do you guys mind if I speak with my dad for a minute?"

"Of course not," said Joe.

"Go ahead," said Ruby.

We got outside in the sunny air. "Want to see around the POW camp?" I asked. We started walking around.

"So Nathan's keys were found here. Why?" he asked.

"I think Tony Zapallero morphed him here," I said, breaking the code of silence.

Dad stopped and looked at me. "That guy is bad news."

I nodded and got up the courage to ask him a loaded question. "Do you remember Zapallero conducting those experiments on you?"

My father's face grew pale. "How did you know about that?"

"Mrs. B told me. She said the only reason I can stop him is because I have your DNA. It's the DNA he based his prototype on," I said.

"There's no way I'm letting that sleazebag near you," said Dad slowly with a steely intensity. He was always so mellow. But now he looked different. My father looked like he was ready to destroy Tony Zapallero.

"We have to stop him," he said.

"Joe made a plan and I think it will work," I said and told him Joe's plan.

CHAPTER FORTY-EIGHT

Time Out

We came back to the bunker and found Joe and Ruby and discussed the plan some more.

"You have the picture, right?" Joe asked after we had gone through everything. He was referring to the Ghetto Swingers picture.

"Yes," I said, patting the picture in my pocket.

"Good, let's focus on the drummer in the band. Let's zap him right into it. Zapallero will see what it's like to suffer for one's art," said Joe. I looked down at the poor drummer and once again remembered the entire poor band's fate. All of them had wound up in the ovens. Zapallero had tried to get Nathan into one of those ovens.

Joe looked at his watch. "We'd better get over to the press conference," he said.

Dad said goodbye and headed back to his car as we had agreed. We didn't want him to draw too much attention. He was going to help us later.

Joe, Ruby and I walked over to the latest press conference where a group had gathered on the grass. We'd been to so many in the past few days that I was beginning to feel like a reporter. I saw Tony Zapallero.

He was here, surrounded by thugs. I recognized that slicked black oiled head of hair anywhere.

The mayor and the police chief started the briefing and were listing the latest findings. The policeman held up a small baggie with a set of keys in it.

And then something unfortunate happened. It started again. The Mayor's voice turned to pitter patter that soon became musical notes. Within seconds, he was singing a heartbreaking rendition of Glenn Miller's infectious hit, "In the Mood."

Before I could stop it, I was musi-morphing again. I was scared. I didn't want this to be happening to me now. I wasn't in control. I stared at the back of Zapallero's head and he turned around, smiling sinisterly. He'd planned this all along.

I was amazed at how fast he worked, planting the music in my brain and in my body. It grew louder and louder and louder. I wanted to get away, but I was stuck to the ground, powerless to move my feet.

I was unable to move anything. The music overtook me, paralyzing me. I tried to see if Joe noticed, but I couldn't even turn my head towards him. My mind was racing at 100 miles per hour even as my body remained as immobile as a statue. What had I been thinking? How could I be a match for this guy?

But then I remembered Joe's plan. I sensed motion next to me. It was Joe pulling out his iPod.

"Don't worry. I'll get you out of this," he whispered. He pulled out the picture of the Ghetto Swingers from his other pocket and started humming under his breath.

The humming was bothering the folks around us. "Shut up! I'm trying to hear this," said one reporter next to Joe.

Joe lowered his voice but still kept humming, but it wasn't strong enough to offset the music Zapallero had programmed in me. I felt an icy jolt course through my veins.

The only thing I could still move were my eyelids, but now I closed my eyes to hum. I knew that was a risk. I knew he could freeze them too and at any moment I might not be able to see. But I had to take the chance.

I summoned up the strength and hummed with Joe. Despite all this chaos that was occurring between the three of us, the press conference seemed to go on like business as usual. Ruby had stepped up into the front row to pay closer attention.

The humming was helping. I wasn't hearing the Glenn Miller song anymore. My own music was fighting Zapallero's soundtrack. Finally, I could move my feet and then my hands.

I turned and smiled at Joe. I saw Zapallero's neck twitch. Did he realize he had lost this round? I didn't want to wait to find out. Joe and I quietly left.

The press conference was ending. Clarinda officials admitted they continued to be totally stumped. No one knew what had happened to Nathan Gordon. The investigation remained open.

Zapallero turned around and was surprised to see us gone and then looked around nervously. He spotted Joe and me by Joe's car.

Zapallero started walking towards us with his thugs wearing a pissed-off look on his face. Ruby and my dad had now joined us by the car.

Zapallero eyed my dad curiously, as if he was trying to figure out how he knew this older long-haired guy. We beckoned for him to follow us around the side of the building that held the bunks.

I held up my hand to stop the thugs who looked right past me at their boss for instructions. "We have to talk with Tony alone," I said, trying to sound cool to conceal the nervousness I felt inside.

Tony laughed. "You think you have anything to say that I don't already know?" he said mockingly.

"Maybe a thing or two," I said.

"I like your spunkiness," Zapallero said. He turned to his thugs. "Fine, let me see what these clowns have to say," he said. "This better be good. I'm very busy, as you know."

"Yeah, we know," said my father.

Zapallero studied him again. "You're that rock star, aren't you?" But as soon as he said it, he realized who my dad was.

He had never put two and two together, but it made sense that the kid would turn out to be someone big in the music industry. He had been a prodigy. This was Dana's kid, the kid he'd mind controlled in that basement so many years ago.

Long forgotten memories flashed before Zapallero as he realized he was standing in front of someone far more powerful than himself. He pulled an iPod out of his pocket and pointed it at all of them. I'm sure he would've zapped every single one of us, except that we were prepared.

Joe, Dad, Ruby and I had already pulled out our own iPods. Tony staggered back a few feet.

"Where'd you get those?" he stammered, his hands shaking. Gone was the cocky Cheshire cat of a few minutes ago.

"We got them from you! We got them at Cougar," I said. I was really enjoying this.

"You think you're so smart and powerful, don't you!" sneered Zapallero.

"I get a lot of that from my father," I said.

Zapallero looked from me to my dad and for the first time made the connection, realizing that I was his daughter. Now he understood how I kept foiling his plans.

"You guys wouldn't be half as powerful as you are if I hadn't shown your dad how to musi-morph in the first place!" Zapallero remarked snidely.

"You wouldn't be half of powerful as you are if it weren't for me," my father said with burning intensity. "You'd be nothing without the power you stole from me."

Zapallero laughed in that hyena-like way of his. "You didn't even know you had it. I've multiplied that power twentyfold. I've expanded that power so much in fact the possibilities of what I can do with it are endless," he said, chuckling sinisterly.

I hated him more now than ever.

"Why don't you join me? We could all make beautiful music together and rule the world!" he said, laughing madly all of a sudden. The laughter turned to music in my head and I felt my resolve easing. We had to move fast or he was going to suck all of us up in his evil musical vortex.

"That'll never happen!" shrieked Ruby and she pressed her iPod and pointed it at Zapallero. We all did the same and started humming my dad's song "Castles." We actually sounded good. Joe had a great voice. What wasn't he good at?

We hummed with every fiber of our beings and waved the picture of the Ghetto Swingers in front of Zapallero's face. In a matter of seconds, he got a glazed look on his face and I knew the cold fusion was starting to take hold.

He tried to move but it appeared like he was struggling, like he was frozen. The paralysis was setting in.

And just like that, it happened. In one second, Zapallero's head swung sideways and then he disappeared in a puff of purple smoke.

"It worked!" gasped Joe.

"Come on. We'd better get out of here before his thugs start looking for him and us," I said.

CHAPTER FORTY-NINE

Last song for Zapallero

Mrs. B told me that Zapallero hadn't been in Musicland for over 30 years. He'd been banned so long ago that at first he was ecstatic to be breaking through the barrier.

But then he realized he wouldn't be landing in a good place or time, and that this time he'd been given a one-way ticket.

After the purple flash had blinded him, he had found himself suspended in utter darkness. It was terrifying to experience firsthand the frightening musical trajectory he had invented. At the end of the interminable dark tunnel, he saw flickering white lights and found himself floating among these lights.

They turned into musical notes and he realized he was skidding over the cosmic treble and bass staff he himself had created. He was floating through music and felt himself being pulled towards a giant pause sign that pulsated like a huge organism in the middle of this intergalactic composition.

He tried to resist the gravity but couldn't as he was dragged into the black hole, the abyss of his own making.

He heard a loud, piercing shriek followed again by utter darkness and silence. Then Mrs. B said Zapallero landed square on his feet on very hard concrete.

He was greeted by a soldier's barking orders. "Achtung!" the clipped voice roared harshly, hurting his ears. Zapallero opened his eyes and was numb with terror. He saw that he was inside a crudely built house. Bunk beds lined the walls. From the beds stared emaciated faces belonging to skeletal people in black and white striped pajamas.

They barely looked human except for the sorrow in their sunken eyes. Zapallero realized he'd landed in a concentration camp.

"Everybody line up. We want to inspect you," the guard barked and a murmur arose through the room.

"This is a selection," whispered a prisoner to the right of Zapallero, and the new head of Cougar Aviation slumped down in despair.

It meant the Nazis would be selecting people to be exterminated in the ovens. Zapallero looked around at the gaunt faces and wondered how these prisoners had done this for so long. How had they stared death in the face for months? In that moment, Zapallero was sorry for all the horrible things he'd done. But he knew it was too late to change or to try to fix things. His eyes met another prisoner's in the bunk.

This man looked familiar and then he realized who he was. Zapallero was staring into the face of John Kiefer.

"Can you help me? Please? I'll give you stock options. I'll give you the whole company," he pleaded.

Kiefer shook his head pityingly.

"You're not supposed to be talking!" said a menacing SS officer, who saw Zapallero whispering. He walked over and viciously cracked a big stick across his shoulders. The pain was excruciating.

"Come with me!" he barked.

Mrs. B said Zapallero knew then that he had been selected. He looked up at Kiefer, who stared back at him with pity as he and other selected inmates were moved out of the bunker and in a line outside a building with a huge chimney that spouted black smoke.

He was pushed roughly inside. SS officers slammed a big metal door on Zapallero and the evil mogul breathed in the unforgettable smell of fear and death. And that was the last smell he would ever know.

CHAPTER FIFTY

Evening the Score

Back in Clarinda, it took us a few moments to recover from seeing Zapallero dissolve into a purple cloud. I wanted to shout with glee, but we had so much to do and little time to do it.

If we pulled off Joe's plan, we knew we had to destroy all of Zap's iPods so that nobody could ever try to use them again. If word got out about how they could be used, we could have a national disaster on our hands.

We sprinted back to the bunker.

"I'll go with Joe," said my dad suddenly, but Ruby would have no part of it.

"I'm going," said Ruby, challenging any of us to dare her.

"You can't," I said. "It's too dangerous. Mrs. B said I had to do this. I'll go alone." We weren't even sure if both of us could go at the same time, using Zapallero's method. But there was no convincing Ruby.

"I don't care. If I can't be with Nathan then there's no point...." said Ruby fighting tears.

Joe chimed in. "It's not safe for any of us, but it might be safer for two of us to go. If something goes wrong, then maybe one of us can try to come back for help," he said.

Ruby held up her iPod and put her finger on the button. "I'll go myself. I don't care," she said.

"Okay Ruby," I said. "It's settled. Ruby and I will go. We've gone to Musicland before and got back okay. This time we'll use the iPods and we should be able to do it."

There was no use in arguing. We had little time. Who knew where Zapallero had programmed Nathan to go next and when? Everything seemed to point to Camp Clarinda. It didn't seem half as dangerous as a concentration camp, but if Zapallero had put Nathan there it couldn't be too safe either.

We all walked to the spot where they had found Nathan's keys on a little table near the bunk beds. There was a photo displayed showing the POWs that had lived there during the war. I looked at the faces of the men in the picture. They were sitting on one of the bunk beds, on the bottom bunk.

I studied them closely and something jumped out at me. My eyes kept travelling to one in particular, who seemed to have a half smile on his face. I had seen that smile before. Slowly, I pulled out the picture of the Ghetto Swingers.

I wasn't looking at the Jewish musicians this time. Instead, I searched the group of German soldiers behind the band. And then I saw it, that smile.

It was the same man in both pictures. One of the German soldiers who had watched the Ghetto Swingers perform had also wound up in Camp Clarinda as a prisoner of war in America. I had taken that smile in the first picture to be a cruel smirk.

But now that I saw him in the Camp Clarinda POW picture, I got a different impression. He looked sad. Maybe he had been sad in the earlier picture too as he watched the Jewish prisoners playing music for the last performance of their lives.

"Joe! Joe! Look!" I exclaimed shaking the photo in my hand at him. "The soldier here is the same guy at Clarinda!"

I felt pity for this soldier all of a sudden. I knew that somehow he was the key. Maybe he had loved the swing. Maybe he'd liked American music. Maybe he'd hated what he had been made to do. Maybe it killed him a little each day when he had to participate in the senseless murder of innocent Jews and other targeted people.

How horrible it must have been to serve in the SS and have a conscience, I thought. I couldn't understand how anyone could live with themselves under those circumstances. I looked from one photo to the other, trying to read the expression in that soldier's eyes.

"We need to look at this photo," I exclaimed, pointing at the Clarinda photo.

"Okay, let's try it then," said Ruby.

"Wait!" exclaimed my father. "I don't want you to go, Zoey."

"We have a lot of catching up to do, Dad. I'll be back. We have to save Nathan," I said, pressing the iPod.

We had no choice now. I'd started the process. Ruby turned on her iPod and we all started humming "Moonlight Serenade" and stared at the soldiers in the POW photo.

I felt the cold searing through my body and looked over at Ruby. She seemed to be shivering as well and then everything went dark.

CHAPTER FIFTY-ONE

Repeat Signs

Nathan was actually so close yet so far at that very moment, in a world an octave away. He was resting in the top bunk of the bunk bed in the photo.

The year was 1944. Rain pelted across the grey Iowa landscape. He looked out his window after a long day's work.

Nathan watched the rain falling on the farm land. It was actually comforting. He'd grown up in farm country like this. But that was another lifetime. He was beginning to feel resigned to the fact that he'd probably spend the rest of his days drifting from era to era in this endless musical time warp.

The POW camp was a big improvement from the concentration camp, but it still wasn't home. And he was so worn down from pretending he was German.

Some of the POWs liked it there. They liked the American food and the people, the music and the movies. But other prisoners were diehard Nazis who would beat him to pulp if they realized he was an imposter.

Many of them acted like they enjoyed America but privately ridiculed the Americans who were so proud for "converting" these German soldiers.

Music had once again been Nathan's salvation during these last few days. He heard it now from down the hall as he gazed out his window. For the millionth time, Nathan swore that if he ever got out of this situation alive, he'd spend more time on his music.

Unable to sleep, he got down from the bunk to get a drink of water from a little kitchen in the back of the building. As soon as he turned on the tap, three hulking inmates walked in menacingly.

"Hey Swing man! You like that American big band stuff, don't you!" said one blonde classically Aryan-looking soldier. His enormous hands were curled into fists. Nathan frowned.

"I don't know what you're talking about," he said. The soldier's heavily muscled body quivered with rage.

"Don't pretend! We know your type. You'd throw everything aside to stay here in America," the soldier growled.

"You stupid man!" he said as his face grew redder with each second.

Suddenly all three POWs lunged at Nathan, swinging their clubbed fists hard at his head. Nathan tried to shield himself with his arms but it was little help against the three of them, who dealt him hard blows to the head and pushed him against the wall.

Nathan took a deep breath and braced himself to get the stuffing beat of him. But then he heard his name.

"Nathan!" He turned and did not believe what he saw. Ruby and I were in Camp Clarinda.

We had landed right in the little kitchen just as the three POWs were about to kick the daylights out of Nathan.

"Leave him alone!" I shrieked. The three gorillas turned to us, clearly startled.

Ruby and I pointed the iPods at them and started to hum and stared into the picture of the Ghetto Swingers. They started flinching as the icy bolt hit them and then within seconds they were gone, disintegrating into a purple puff of smoke.

"Ruby!" exclaimed Nathan, rushing towards her. They embraced. Ruby was crying and Nathan had tears in his eyes. They began to kiss.

Embarrassed, I turned away to give them some privacy.

"Thank you," said Nathan now standing in front of me, holding Ruby's hand.

"I'm so glad we finally found you!" I said, fighting back tears of my own. "Come on, let's get back in case Zapallero has pre-programmed you to go somewhere else," I said.

I silently thanked Joe for thinking ahead to this part. He had grabbed brochures from the modern day museum in Clarinda for each of us before we left. I gave Ruby and Nathan iPods and a brochure.

"Just do as we do," I said to Nathan. He nodded, looking mystified.

We all stared at the brochure and hummed "Take Me Home, Country Roads," by John Denver, another amazing artist who had perished in the sky. Joe had found it among Zapallero's playlist. Denver was a prolific songwriter with huge hits like "Sunshine on My Shoulders." He was also a great photographer, humanitarian and an avid pilot and was only fifty-three when he crashed into the Pacific Ocean.

I could only imagine what Zap's plans would have been for that song, but by using the imagery from Clarinda, we hoped the song would literally "take us home" and not aboard Denver's fatal flight.

Nathan, Ruby and I pushed the buttons on our iPods. We felt jolted by the cold fusion and then everything went dark.

I closed my eyes and held my breath, praying that Joe's plan worked. When I opened them again, I felt so relieved. We were back at Clarinda in the present.

CHAPTER FIFTY-TWO

Wedding Bell Blues

The wedding took place later that summer in the hangar where it all began. The building had been transformed into a beautiful ballroom with dazzling flowers, warm glowing candles and a bountiful buffet. Dad, Joe and I were providing the music in the far corner. But right now, we were quietly watching the ceremony.

Ruby looked amazing in her white lace gown and crown of white flowers. Nathan looked distinguished in his tuxedo. They glowed.

Tammy and Dan were in the procession. Tammy fought back tears. Throughout this ordeal, we had become family. We'd witnessed horrible evil at the hand of Zapallero and others in war.

I would never be the same. My piano playing would never be the same. Seeing a senseless, violent loss of life will do that to an artist, to anybody. But no doubt this experience would inform my playing.

For through it all there was the music. And there was flight. I saw death but I also saw a fire that burned brightly. I saw how dreams can keep a person alive. I saw how some people breathe the air they breathe in so that can do the things they love. They live for that mainly, that thing they love. A pilot's heart is always in the sky.

I learned that love, the love of flight, I realized as I glanced at the other members of this wonderful trio. These two players were my favorite guys in the world. Nathan was a close third.

"I am going to set you up with my buddy who's a flight instructor out of Los Angeles," said Nathan during the rehearsal dinner the night before. "And I'm treating!"

How incredible was that? Flying lessons were expensive. It would be great to learn to fly, I thought. We were sitting quietly now in the corner watching the ceremony.

After their vows, Nathan took Ruby's face in his hands and kissed her long and tenderly. "I'd travel to the end of time for you," he whispered to her.

Everyone clapped and cried. Then my father, Joe and I played song after song after song by great artists who died in flight but remained forever airborne through their music.

The End